"My assignment is Valentine's Day…and romance," Jud added. "Maybe you can help me."

He tapped her business card against his glass. Grace Harrison, Matchmaker for Individuals Seeking Faith-Based Romance.

Grace imagined the headlines swirling through his reporter's brain. Senator's Daughter Plays the Dating Game. Love—Washington-Style.

"I doubt it."

"Well, if you don't want people to know about your matchmaking program—one that could change their lives…"

She studied him, trying to come to a decision. "You have to understand that I don't trust the media, Mr. Marlowe. If I agree to be a resource for your story on matchmaking, my father is off-limits."

"Are there other rules?"

She took a deep breath, having just made a decision she hoped she would not regret. The program could use the publicity. "If you're truly interested in a story on the program, perhaps you should come observe how it works for yourself."

Books by Anna Schmidt

Love Inspired

Caroline and the Preacher #72
A Mother for Amanda #109
The Doctor's Miracle #146
Love Next Door #294
Matchmaker, Matchmaker... #333

ANNA SCHMIDT

has been writing most of her life. Her first "critical" success was a short poem she wrote for a Bible study class in fourth grade. Several years later she launched her career as a published author with a two-act play and several works of nonfiction. Anna is a transplanted Virginian, living now in Wisconsin. She has worked in marketing and public relations for two international companies, and enjoys traveling, gardening, long walks in the city or country and antiquing. She has written five novels for Steeple Hill—one of which was a finalist for the coveted RITA® Award given by Romance Writers of America. Anna would love to "meet" her readers—feel free to contact her online at www.booksbyanna.com.

MATCHMAKER, MATCHMAKER...
ANNA SCHMIDT

Steeple
Hill®

Published by Steeple Hill Books™

STEEPLE HILL BOOKS

Steeple Hill®

ISBN 0-373-87345-X

MATCHMAKER, MATCHMAKER…

This edition published by arrangement with Steeple Hill Books.

® and TM are trademarks of Steeple Hill Books, used under license. Trademarks indicated with ® are registered in the United States Patent and Trademark Office, the Canadian Trade Marks Office and in other countries.

www.SteepleHill.com

Printed in U.S.A.

I keep Yahweh before me always,
for with Him at my right hand,
nothing can shake me.
—*Psalms* 16:8

For Louise and Earle
Clara and Alex

Chapter One

Inside the Capitol, the high domed walls of the rotunda echoed with conversation. Members of Congress—new and experienced—along with their staffs and families, accepted refreshments from trays offered by uniformed waiters. Grace Harrison helped herself to a glass of the watery punch and strolled the perimeter of the crowded gathering, eyes and ears on alert.

As the daughter of one of the nation's most popular senators, Grace was an expert at handling the media and especially at spotting any reporter who might be specifically looking for a story on her family. Riley Harrison had taught her well. He had also pleaded with her to show up at this welcoming reception. Her assignment was to help the rest of his staff keep the press at bay while he worked the room.

"Dad," Grace had said, knowing that she didn't need to finish her plea. Her father was well aware of her aversion to any sort of political function. Fortunately, the public was completely sympathetic to her desire to have a normal life outside the spotlight. They even applauded her efforts. They loved the fact that she still lived at home with her parents and embraced her no-nonsense style and her choice to pursue her career as a religious education and program director for one of the city's oldest churches. She was viewed as more normal and more in touch with the public than most offspring of politicians—and that translated into increased popularity and votes for her father.

"Now, Gracie, I know you hate these things, but it's been a while since I asked you to do anything like this and the media will love it."

Grace sightings were a real coup for any D.C. reporter. In spite of their respect for her preference to lead a quiet life, the public ate up any news about Grace. Most recently the Washington press had had a field day speculating on the breakup of her long romance with a high profile attorney. The simple explanation was that she and Nick had both realized they were together more out of habit and a friendship that dated back to their high school days. But that was far too mundane for the newsman to accept without two days of rumors and stories of a heartbroken Grace.

When Nick began dating Grace's best friend Bethany, the news fueled a fresh wave of rumors and conjecture. Fortunately the election had turned attention away from Grace and on to the possibility of meatier news. It was ironic that in trying to maintain a low profile and get on with her life, she had become material for the gossipmongers.

"But, Dad…"

"Ken's wife went into labor an hour ago, honey. You know that I wouldn't ask otherwise. I really need your help. An hour—that's it, I promise."

Ken was the senator's chief of staff and more than once he had persuaded her father that Grace's preference for a life of her own out of the spotlight, was a definite plus with the voters. She owed him. "Okay. One hour," she agreed, although she knew that it would be at least two.

Grace did her duty, mingling with members of Congress who had been old family friends for years and introducing herself to the newcomers who were clearly delighted to meet the elusive daughter of Senator Riley Harrison.

Grace knew most of the press, so she spotted the new guy right away. She leaned against a marble column and crossed one ankle over the other as she studied him. If she hadn't seen the press badge, she might have assumed he was a staffer for a member of the new class of Congress.

Even in terms of being a journalist, he looked more like a seasoned veteran than a rookie. The less experienced reporters could never completely conceal their eagerness and excitement at having landed an assignment to cover their first event on the Hill. This guy looked anything but eager or excited. He looked jaded, even a little hostile, as if anticipating the event to be a complete flop in terms of yielding anything of use to him. He strolled around the perimeter of the room, with an air of nonchalance, but his eyes scanned the crowd with practiced skill. He wasn't yet sure what he was looking for, but everything about him told Grace that he could recognize even the slightest indication of a story.

She recorded his physical features—six feet, athletic build, clothes selected as much for the air of casual cool as their perfect fit. But it was the face that drew her attention. Charcoal hair that might gray prematurely to salt-and-pepper in a few years, eyes deep-set and vigilant, watching everyone and everything in his surroundings, skin that would sport an intriguing five o'clock shadow by three and a mouth that promised a dimple when, and if, he smiled.

He didn't appear to have noticed her, or if he had, he was playing it very cool. Grace was used to being recognized and had no doubt that he would be no exception. She paused as he ambled closer. Then she saw him recognize her father. His body posture changed to a predatory readiness and his eyes brightened like a hunter who had just spotted a sixteen-point buck. Grace scanned the room and saw the other members of her father's staff occupied with reporters from the other papers and local television stations. This one was hers. She sighed, pushed herself away from the cool marble of the column and stepped directly in his path.

"Hi," she said with a bright, if completely artificial, smile. He glanced at her. His eyes flickered with recognition, but to her surprise he offered an equally artificial smile and prepared to move on. "Quite a crowd," she added, raising her voice to be heard above the clamor in the cavernous rotunda. She moved closer, effectively trapping him between a marble column, the bust of Thomas Jefferson, and herself.

It was obvious that he knew who she was. However, the only thing she saw clearly reflected in those deepset eyes—which she now saw were a steely gray—was that she was in his way. Grace waited as he waged the battle between innate politeness and the need to keep tracking his prey—her father, in this case. Politeness won.

"Yes, quite a crowd. Seems like everyone is here except the President and his entourage." His smile was so tight that the dimple never appeared and he looked over her instead of at her. It was evident that he hoped that she'd get the message and move on.

She checked the name on his press badge—Jud Marlowe—and realized she knew the name but not the man. She tried to think how his name might have come up. He shifted slightly in order to see around her and the column as he continued to track her father. *That* Jud Marlowe.

Marlowe was the reporter who had written a scathing expose on Charlie Blackwell, a former business partner of her father's and a dear family friend. Marlowe was the one who had accepted documents and other information from a supposedly trusted source without realizing that his source had her own agenda when it came to ruining Charlie. In an effort to save face and avoid a huge lawsuit, the paper had fired him.

Grace frowned and sipped her punch. Obviously, he'd gotten himself rehired. She glanced at the press badge again. *Washington Today*. Millie Peterson's paper. That made sense. Millie had worked hard to put together a staff of slightly renegade journalists who weren't afraid to go after a story on the slimmest of information.

"Would you excuse me?" he said, starting to make his move, his attention still firmly on her father through the gathering.

Grace wasn't about to allow this guy within ten feet of her father. She shifted positions, making it impossible for him to leave without physically pushing her aside, and said, "I'm Grace Harrison."

He gave her his full attention for the first time since she initiated contact. "I know," he replied and said nothing more. Instead he studied her, clearly trying to figure out why the reclusive Grace Harrison had actually introduced herself to a reporter.

Jud Marlowe had been with the Washington, D.C. newspaper nearly six weeks before he got his first big assignment to attend a function at the Capitol.

This is it, he thought when managing editor Millie Peterson called him into her office—the chance to show them what I can do.

"Think of it as a rite of initiation," Millie told him. "I want you to be on the lookout for a possible angle for a Valentine's Day feature."

Valentine's Day? Jud bit his lip to keep from shouting it. Millie was testing him, as she had been since she hired him. Just how far could she push him before he stepped over the line—again?

"Something not too warm and fuzzy—we like edgy around here," she had added as if this were his first day at the paper.

If Valentine's Day with an edge was what Millie wanted, he was determined to be the man to give it to her. And although he had his doubts that the Capitol function would really yield pay dirt, he was willing to play the good soldier and follow the lead.

The occasion was a reception following the swearing-in of the newly elected freshmen class of the Congress. "The new members might as well be wearing signs," Millie had instructed. "They'll stand out. Look for things like which old-timers are courting which newcomers. Look for staff members who are just a little too attached to their bosses. Look for—"

"Got it," Jud had interrupted as he headed for the door. He'd really had it with Peterson's "coaching," as she called it. Treating him more like a rookie with no experience was more like it.

Valentine's schmalintine's, he thought as he scanned the room. He was here for a story—hard news. He had a career to redeem and if he couldn't find something to make Millie forget all about Valentine's Day in this gathering, then he might as well start looking for some other way to make a living.

The problem was the senator's daughter had attached herself to him like a leech. He tried politeness, which did not work at all. He knew exactly who she was and her presence at this event—given her reputation for avoiding political functions—spoke volumes about the fact that something was going on. He was well aware that any other reporter in the room would be thrilled at being targeted by Grace Harrison, whatever her motive. He wasn't going to fall for it. The problem was how to ditch her so he could concentrate on her father. He couldn't catch a break.

He was about to gently squeeze past her and move on when she said, "I'm Grace Harrison."

"I know."

Jud looked directly at her for the first time since she'd accosted him, curious as to why she was so desperate to keep him occupied that she would actually introduce herself. Her face was upturned because of the difference in heights, so the first thing he noticed were the most incredible pair of blue eyes he'd ever seen. Or maybe it was the magnified effect of a pair of wire-rimmed glasses that were completely wrong for the petite woman's gamine face. Jud waited to see what she'd do next.

She offered her hand, "And you are…" She squinted at his press badge.

"Jud Marlowe," he said, liking the firmness of her grip in spite of the delicacy of her small-boned hand. "Asking the obvious question," he said, "it's *that* Harrison, right?" He nodded in the direction of the portly man who was surrounded by an admiring circle.

He was stalling for time while he mentally organized the facts. Grace Harrison, who rarely made public appearances of any sort, was here at an event that ranked somewhere near the cellar in terms of political and social importance. Most of the media outlets had opted to sit this one out. There wasn't a "name" reporter in the place. Grace had singled him out and made a deliberate approach.

There's a story here somewhere, Marlowe. Grace Harrison already knows what it is, and she's working overtime to be sure you don't get any closer to finding out.

Jud couldn't wait to drop this little jewel on Millie Peterson's desk. He could practically hear her handing off her dumb Valentine's assignment to one of the wannabes as he pursued whatever Grace was trying to cover up. He made every attempt to control his joy.

He took a long swallow of his punch as he sized up the petite woman who suddenly seemed to be struggling for small talk that might keep him busy. He refused to help her out, using the time to mentally record details about her. She was about five-four, weighed maybe 110 pounds, had short, professionally cut and styled brown hair, good cheekbones and lips that could use some color. Nothing there of particular interest. But the eyes were something altogether different. They belied the friendly smile and greeting. They probed and questioned and made no apology in the process.

Forget the looks. Real deal or a phony?

Grace Harrison was, in his opinion, most definitely the real deal—what you saw was what you got with her. He'd stake what was left of his career on that.

"You're new," she continued, sipping her punch and studying him over the rims of her glasses.

"Does it show?" He patted himself down as if searching for some obvious sign. She looked puzzled when he'd expected a laugh.

Her smile, which was now definitely phony, wavered. "Oh, that's a joke, right? I meant that you're new to D.C.—to the Hill at least."

He completed his profile of her by checking out her clothes. Quality, but she was definitely in need of a fashion makeover. Her clothes were obviously name-brand stuff, but the style had gone out of fashion at least a couple of seasons earlier. The suit was expensive and fit her well, but it was a really boring shade of gray that did absolutely nothing for her. In the right clothes and with a little makeup, she had the makings of a knockout.

He pointed to his press badge. "*Washington Today*—Metro-slash-Lifestyle." He had no idea why he'd added his position at the paper.

"Really? I would have guessed the national or even foreign news desk." Her tone left little doubt that she had really hoped he had come just for the punch and store-bought cookies.

He continued to speculate as to why Grace would voluntarily introduce herself to anyone wearing a press credential.

Put her at ease, Marlowe.

"*Washington Today* is a pretty bare-bones operation—at least when it comes to staff—when compared to the *Post* or others in that elite league. We take whatever assignments we're given. Although I'm sure I would have been on the A-list for this event anyway. I have friends in high places."

Again, the slightly puzzled frown followed the hesitant smile as if she'd just realized he was joking. "No doubt," she agreed, nodding her head sagely.

She's defrosting, Marlowe. Keep working it.

"It's true," he insisted. "A good friend works for the congresswoman from Idaho."

"But surely you can see your friend in better places than this. My guess is that you're here for a story. What's the angle? Election reform? Medicare?"

"Valentine's Day."

That caught her completely off guard. "At the Capitol?" She smiled uncertainly. "You're joking again, right?"

He shrugged. "You never know where a good lead on romance might turn up. Take that twosome over there. Heads all bent low, practically whispering sweet nothings in each other's ear, casting their eyes over the room to be sure they aren't discovered."

"You may be new to D.C., but I'm guessing that you know those two are more likely plotting a coup than snuggling," Grace replied and this time there was no hesitation in her smile. "As you no doubt know, that's Senator Maxine Lockwood and the Speaker of the House, both members of the erstwhile 'loyal opposition.' Let's see…" She surveyed the room for a few seconds, seeking a more valid example of romance.

"Okay. Then, we might talk about your father, who certainly seems to be romancing the new members of the Congress—in a completely political, non-romantic way, I mean." Might as well see how she responds, he thought as the gathering around her father laughed loudly at something the senator said before he moved on to the next group of colleagues. Harrison glanced at his daughter and nodded. There was no reason for him to notice Jud. In spite of Jud's story, the two had never met.

Grace surprised him by leaning close as she set her empty punch cup on the tray of a passing waiter. In one smooth motion she took hold of his arm and turned him so his back was to her father. "You're wasting your time with my father. Now, if it's romance you want, that couple over there might have some potential." She nodded toward two congressional staffers. "Notice the eye contact. The way they seem totally unaware of anyone else."

"But, are they anybody?" He hadn't missed her deliberate attempt to divert his attention from her father. What's that about? All of his journalistic instincts were on high alert. He didn't know why yet, but he was sure that he had just accidentally fallen into something that could change his future big-time. Stick with her. Follow the lead—in this case, follow the lady.

"Of course, they're somebody," she said with a hint of irritation that brought his attention immediately back to the business at hand.

"Hey, you know how it goes in my business. Names sell papers."

"Oh, you want news, as in scandal or gossip. How about a bit of good old-fashioned mudslinging?" Her eyes flashed. "And here I thought you said that the assignment was romance."

"The assignment is Valentine's Day," he corrected her, trying to stem his own irritation. Calm down, Jud. You're ticking her off. He grinned. "*And* romance," he added.

"*And* politics," she said, obviously having decided to calm down a little as well.

"That, too."

"Then that couple could be perfect. They don't have the name power you may want, but what if it was a sort of Mary Matalin and James Carville match? Only this time she's the liberal and he's the conservative?" She was clearly warming to her subject. "Imagine the drama. Can love truly conquer all?"

"You're good at this." He couldn't help being intrigued that she'd elected to divert his attention from her father by offering ideas for his story. It was naïve but charming,

But it wasn't going to work on a veteran reporter like Jud.

She produced a card from the small suede clutch purse she carried. "Actually I'm something of a professional."

Jud was sure that she'd decided to deliberately misinterpret him. He had meant that she was good at diverting attention from her father. He read the card.

Grace Harrison, Matchmaker for Individuals Seeking Faith-Based Romance.

"You're a matchmaker? Like in *Hello, Dolly?*"

"Something like that."

"You're kidding." Could this day get any better? Grace Harrison, the lead to the senator and a Valentine's angle all neatly wrapped in one package. Millie was going to have a cow over this one.

"I have a good sense of humor, Mr. Marlowe, but I rarely go to the trouble of backing it up with phony business cards."

"So, this dating service…"

Once again, she stiffened slightly and the light in her eyes flickered. "I am a matchmaker and we offer a program to match young professionals who are serious about establishing a long-lasting relationship. It is *not* a dating service." She spoke those last two words as if they had left a horrible taste in her mouth.

"My mistake. I wasn't aware that today's young professionals were in need of a matchmaker, especially here in D.C. where eight out of ten people might well fit into the 'young professional' category."

"You'd be surprised. It seems the busier and more successful a man or woman is, the less time they have to devote to finding that special relationship."

"Define 'special relationship.'"

"One where both parties are committed for the long term, where most likely they are ready to marry and build a life with a partner."

Jud studied the card again. "And the 'faith-based' piece of it?"

"Participants in the program are all people who believe that their faith is at the very foundation of every decision they make."

Jud knew that by reputation Senator Harrison was a man of strong religious beliefs. He supposed it made sense that the daughter would go one of two ways—follow in her father's footsteps or rebel against her up-bringing. Clearly, Grace had opted for the former. "You don't look like the matchmaker type," he said.

She smiled and this time the smile was genuine. "Oh, I wasn't aware there was a 'type.' Enlighten me, please."

"I don't know. I would have thought more…flamboyant perhaps. Maybe a feather boa. At least a large feathered hat. And you're probably too thin."

"That's quite an imagination you have, Mr. Marlowe."

He was beginning to enjoy this. All the ingredients were coming together. He even had found the perfect slant for Millie's precious Valentine's assignment. On top of that he was standing next to the one person who could lead him straight to any breaking news about the always interesting Senator Riley Harrison.

"Please call me Jud."

Grace took a moment to consider whether accepting him on a first-name basis was going too far.

"Okay, Jud. It seems to me that deciding what a person should dress and look like depending on one's career could get in the way of objective reporting."

She saw that she had hit a nerve with the reference

to objective reporting. Would he realize that she'd recognized his name the moment she'd seen his press badge? Grace watched as he weighed the risk of losing his temper against the potential for a story that included her. His next comment made it obvious that the story had won.

"Speaking of Valentine angles," he said, deliberately changing the subject, "maybe you can help me with my story?" He tapped her business card against the lip of his punch cup.

Grace imagined the headlines swirling through his brain. *Senator's Daughter Hosts the Dating Game. Love—Washington Style. Senator's Little Girl Mends Hearts All Over Town.*

"I doubt it."

"I meant through your service...program."

"Sure you did." She frowned.

Grace was sure that he'd been told more than once that the smile plus a boyish shrug could work wonders on women.

"Well, if you don't want people to know about something this special, a program that could potentially change their lives for the better..."

"I don't think it would be a good idea," she said. "There are confidentiality issues to be considered. I mean people don't usually want it widely known that they're using a matchmaker. Of course, our program is a little different in that it's a group."

"Group dating?" He was working hard to keep a straight face.

"No," she snapped. "It's a program designed for single people to meet other single people just like a dozen other such programs around the city."

Overreacting again.

Jud held up his hands in a sign of surrender. "Sorry. That was out of line."

Grace took a deep breath and willed herself to maintain control. "On the other hand, how unusual that I would be here today and meet this reporter looking for a story on romance," she said, more to herself than to him.

She studied him, trying to come to a decision. "You have to understand that I don't trust the media, Mr. Marlowe," she said, reverting to his full name.

"I never would have guessed," he said and then quickly added, "Joking."

She nodded. "On the other hand, spreading the word on the program could be a good thing. I can see that." She squinted up at him. "Let me think about it."

She was well aware that it really wasn't her call. If he decided to go after the story there wouldn't be a lot she could do to stop him, especially since her father was one of the country's most famous guardians of freedom of the press.

"Of course, there would be some ground rules," she added, deciding to test the waters further.

"For example?"

"If I agree to be a resource for a story on matchmaking, my father is off-limits."

Jud took a moment. "As someone who was raised in

the world of politics, you know that I can't make that promise," he said.

"My father has absolutely no ties to the program. That rule stands." She was so sure that his real target was to get to her father through her that she thought he would give up.

"Are there other rules?"

Tougher than I thought.

Grace pointed to the card. "Faith-based is a prerequisite, not a gimmick. This is not your normal singles club. People who join are serious about finding the right person. They are ready to settle down and they have standards that are rooted in their faith. I won't have you making them look like contestants on one of those horrendous reality TV specials."

Jud grinned. "Why don't you tell me what you really think of those reality shows?" She didn't return his smile. Jud glanced down at her card again. "But why limit it to 'faith-based'? Isn't that discriminating?"

"Not at all. Our program is ecumenical. Because when two people believe in God, I mean, really believe.... Do you believe in God, Jud?"

He took a moment to process the deliberately abrupt change in conversational direction. "Sure," he replied quickly.

Way too flippant. Probably hasn't darkened the door of a church in months, if not years.

Grace shook her head vigorously. "Please don't blow off the question. I'm not talking about believing in the *concept* of God. I'm asking if you believe that a higher power drives your life or is available to do that if you make the right choices?"

"Oh, you want credentials," he said with a smile. "My parents started taking me to church with them about two weeks after I was born. When I got too noisy for sitting through the regular service, I started in the nursery and worked my way up to president of the senior high fellowship. In college—which, by the way, was a private church-supported institution—I attended chapel every morning and vespers every evening. I sang in the choir. I ushered. I was president of the youth group. I attended church camp every summer, and I...."

"Impressive," she interrupted. She looked at him for a second longer, trying to decide whether or not to believe him. "It doesn't really answer the question, but I'll give you benefit of the doubt."

"Oh, thanks. Tell me, do you audition all reporters or am I just lucky?"

He's nearing the breaking point, but he'll hang in there because at the moment he needs me way more than I need him.

She took a deep breath, having just made a decision she hoped she wouldn't regret. Everyone deserved a second chance. The program could use the publicity. So why not? "Let's start with this—if you're truly interested in a story on the program, perhaps you should come observe how it works." She reached out and took the business card she'd handed him and turned it over. "We're at the church coffeehouse every Tuesday at seven."

Chapter Two

After Grace placed her card back in his hand, Jud saw her attention drawn to a stunning redhead, signaling her from across the crowded rotunda. Grace started working her way through the crowd. Jud frowned as he watched several people step forward to greet her.

What gives with this woman? Didn't I say that I was interested in doing a piece on her little dating game—excuse me, matchmaking program?

Then it hit him. Grace was making a point. If he wanted to do a story, it would not only be on her terms, it would be on her turf. He smiled. The woman had obviously learned a lot from her father.

"Whoa, Jud, you've been here less than twenty minutes and already you're moving in on Grace Harrison?" David Forrester raised his eyebrows in mock disapproval, then laughed and clapped Jud on the back. "I'm surprised to see her here. Usually she avoids these things like the plague."

Which begs the question of why is she here and talking to me—a member of the fourth estate, Jud thought.

"Do you know Grace?" he asked his former college roommate. "I mean other than by reputation or through her father?"

David actually blushed. "Well, yeah, sort of. It's a little complicated. Hey, let's hit the buffet before it's all gone," David suggested, steering Jud toward a quieter part of the vast rotunda, where more waiters staffed tables laden with a variety of finger food.

"So, how do you know her?" Jud prompted, wondering why he blushed at the mention of Grace's name.

"I met Grace at the same time I met Suni," he said after they had filled small plates with cheese canapés and fruit skewered to oversize toothpicks. Suni Ashraff was the daughter of the Sri Lankan ambassador. David had been dating her for a couple of months. "I've been meaning to mention Grace to you."

"Not interested," Jud said immediately and was puzzled by David's blank look. "As in 'not interested in seeing her socially.' She's not my type and I'm not ready even if she was." In the short time that David had been seeing Suni, like most people in love, he seemed especially determined to share his good fortune with all his friends.

"No, not that. Not that it wouldn't be a good idea, I mean for you to settle down, but Grace and you? I just don't see it."

"Thanks for the vote of confidence," Jud replied. "I'm thinking of doing a story on…"

Jud stopped filling his plate with cheese and crackers and looked at his bestfriend. "You wanted me to meet Grace, *the matchmaker,* right? That's where you met Suni, isn't it? You said you met her at church so I just assumed you meant church services, but you joined Grace's matchmaking program, didn't you?"

Deep red splotches colored David's cheeks again, but his tone was defensive. "Well, I've done okay, haven't I? I wouldn't cast stones until you've tried it, pal."

"Hey, whatever works." Jud continued to eat and process this new bit of information. If Grace knew David—and if she liked David—then maybe it would give him an advantage. "Is that why you've never wanted to double with me? Afraid I would find out about the matchmaking thing?"

"Not really. See, the thing is that Suni has lived most of her life here in America. She wants to stay here, settle down here for good."

"Okay. That's a good thing, right?"

"Do you know much about Sri Lanka?"

"I know it's been a political and economic hotbed for some time," Jud replied.

"Suni's dad wants her to marry—he even doesn't mind if she marries an American, which is where Grace and the program come in. On the other hand, he wants to be very sure about that future husband so he's set up this rule that most of the time when we go out, unless it's to the church or during the day, we have to have... company."

"A chaperone?" Jud was incredulous. "You *cannot* be serious."

"Oh yeah, I'm serious. Suni tells her dad that he's like a throwback to the Dark Ages, but he told her she could think what she likes, but having been here for a number of years, he knows that some American men have less than scrupulous motives when it comes to choosing their women."

"Meaning?"

"Suni's family has money—a lot of it—mostly from her mother's side. If you ask me, her father is just putting me through what he had to go through to win her mother. Either way, those are his terms, so we're living with them."

"You're telling me that you can't go anywhere with her on your own? Even for coffee?"

David smiled. "Well, it's not quite that medieval, but if we want to go out for dinner or a movie or something, Grace comes along. It kind of limits things, you know? Suni and I feel so guilty always calling on her—not that she ever objects. She's been incredible, and we've become good friends."

Jud worked hard to hide the idea that popped into mind with that bit of information. "So Grace is pretty much tagging along whenever you and Suni date?" David nodded and Jud scraped up the rest of his taco dip with a carrot stick and frowned.

"What?" David asked. "I know that look and it usually means you're cooking up a plan—and forgive me, Jud, but more often than not your plans can lead to trouble."

"Hey, I might be able to help."

"How?" David asked suspiciously.

"Well, Peterson gave me a test. I have to come up with a Valentine's Day feature. Something with an edge, to use her words."

"You're joking," David said with a snort of laughter.

"Do I look like I'm joking?" Jud demanded.

"Okay. Got it. This is serious. So where do Suni and I fit in?"

"If I focus the Valentine piece on how you and Suni met through Grace's program and how her old-fashioned parents accepted you because of the program and how love bloomed and blossomed, et cetera…."

"And you get what out of this?"

"I get to tell your story," Jud replied as if David hadn't been paying attention.

"And?" David pressed.

Jud sighed. He could fool a lot of people a lot of the time, but David knew him too well. "I get to tag along on your dates and be around Grace Harrison."

"You *are* interested. Wow, I would never have thought she was your type." David looked across the room to where Grace was talking to her father.

"Get serious. She's news—I can't say what news yet, but there isn't a reporter in this city who wouldn't sell his grandmother for a chance to hang out with her and win her trust."

David turned his attention back to Jud. He looked disappointed. "Can't do it, my friend," he said and his tone left little room for argument, which didn't stop Jud for a second.

"Why not? You said yourself that you felt guilty imposing on Grace and she probably feels something like a third wheel herself. Think how much more normal things would be if I came along. Two couples out for dinner and a show or going ice skating or—"

David moved a step closer and although he was smiling, his voice was low and dead serious. "Get this straight, I am not going to help you try to dig up dirt on Grace or her father by hanging out with her. She's way too special and he's one of the good guys. Besides, Suni and I owe her everything, including our loyalty."

"Okay. Okay. Relax."

Conversation between them died as they each scanned the room and waited out the other.

"So, why does Suni's family trust Grace?" Jud finally asked. "I mean she's a little young to be in the matchmaking business."

"The two families have known each other since Grace and Suni attended the same high school. Suni's parents trust Grace and with good reason. Her program has been enormously successful in helping couples carefully screen potential life partners."

Jud cupped his free hand like a microphone. "This paid political announcement has been brought to you by another convert to the Grace Harrison program to match lost souls."

David slugged Jud's arm hard. "Be serious, okay?"

"Sorry. You and Suni have found true love. Sounds like a Valentine's story to me."

"Yeah, maybe." David sighed heavily as they made

their way through small knots of politicians toward the exit. "It might be a great story, but one without a happy ending."

"Meaning?"

"Suni's father recently got word that he's due to be called back home by his government any time now. Suni might have no choice but to go with them. Her father doesn't like the idea of her being on her own for a lot of reasons—personal and political. He's afraid something might happen to her."

"That's tough, Dave. I'm really sorry." Jud sincerely wished that he had connections that could make a difference for his friend. "Couldn't the senator help?" He had connections. "Maybe Suni's parents could stay here as well."

"Maybe." David didn't sound convinced, but then his eyes lit up and he smiled. "On the other hand, if you did the story and it featured Suni and me, maybe it would get things on a fast track and Suni would be able to stay because there would be no turning back."

"Isn't that pretty close to what I just said a few minutes ago?" Jud said, jokingly.

"Hey, I thought you wanted to help."

"I do. Grace invited me to stop by the church Tuesday night and check things out. Let's see how that goes."

David looked as if he might actually hug Jud. "It could just work, you know? Thanks, Jud. Wait'll I tell Suni." He pulled his cell phone out of the inner pocket of his suit coat and flipped it open, but stopped short of punching in Suni's number. "Look, I'm trusting you that this won't turn into some kind of Grace Harrison hunt, okay?"

Jud hesitated, then nodded. David grinned, clapped him on the back and then practically ran toward an exit, his cell phone already to his ear. Jud hadn't counted on this particular complication. David was his best friend. David knew him better than anyone. David could cramp his style big-time if he held him to the promise not to turn this story into a focus on Grace—and her father.

I'll make him understand when the time comes, Jud thought.

For the moment he needed to focus on how he could turn a chance meeting with the famous daughter of the renowned senator to his advantage.

Chance meeting? He might be new to D.C., but everyone inside and outside the beltway knew that when Grace Harrison showed up at any political event, it was because her father had asked her to be there. The question was why this event?

After leaving Jud, Grace saw Senator Mark Gordon approaching her father. She started across the room toward her friend Bethany, but caught her father's eye.

"Grace," he boomed just as Gordon reached him. He put one arm around Gordon's shoulders and then motioned for Grace to join them. "Grace, come over here and say hello."

Grace knew exactly what her father wanted. She took her time working her way through the crowded room, pausing two or three times to accept the greetings of people who had heard her father call her and been surprised to see her there. All the while her father and Senator Gordon appeared to be exchanging small talk as they watched her make her way toward them.

When she finally reached them, her father leaned down and kissed her cheek and then introduced her to Senator Gordon, who shook her hand, made a couple of polite comments and then moved on to work the room.

"Perfect, you're a pro at this. We might have to consider running you one of these days," her father said with a grin.

"Not in *my* lifetime," Grace replied, then asked in a softer tone. "How did it go?"

"We made some progress. You know that these things take time. Thanks, honey. I couldn't have done it without your help."

In his plea to get her to attend the function, her father had finally confided that Senator Gordon was seriously considering switching parties. If he did, it would give her father's party a solid majority in the Senate. It would also open all sorts of doors for getting major legislation passed, since Senator Gordon was almost as powerful and respected as Grace's father was. Her father very much needed to talk to Gordon, and had decided that the least likely place to draw attention or start rumors was a public function like the reception.

"Nothing like hiding in plain sight," the senator said with a laugh.

"You owe me," Grace said as she walked arm in arm with her father toward an exit. "Big-time. I had to offer the possibility of a story on the matchmaking program to keep that new reporter's attention away from you." She indicated Jud, who at that point, was deep in conversation with David Forrester.

Her father laughed. "Oh, no, the ultimate price—a reporter doing a story on you! I'll never hear the end of this one, will I?"

"It's not a story on me," Grace grumbled. "It's on the program—or at least it had better be."

"It's a good program, Gracie." Her father hugged her. "And you know how to handle the press better than most. That guy doesn't stand a chance." He kissed the top of her head and raised his hand in greeting to the Speaker of the House. "Got to go, sweetie. See you at home."

"Okay," Grace replied, but her attention wasn't on her father. It was on Jud Marlowe, who headed for another exit, then looked back as if he felt her watching him. He grinned and waved, then fished a cell phone out of his pocket and punched in a number as he walked quickly down the hall.

What have I done? she thought.

Jud started to call his editor to brief her on what had happened, then decided against it. Millie Peterson had given him an assignment. She had also warned him about "hot dogging" as she called it. The assignment was Valentine's Day—warm and fuzzy but with an edge. He wasn't to try to turn it into something more.

Warm and fuzzy was not at all what came to mind when Jud thought of Millie. She was a female version of the stereotypical hardened newsroom veteran. Close-cropped hair with thick bangs cut too short, exposing her unplucked eyebrows. She often wore an oversize man's shirt tucked into pinstriped trousers with a matching jacket draped over the back of her chair. She rarely smiled and Jud would not have been surprised to see her chewing on a fat cigar. Still, he had jumped at the chance to work with her even if the first available opening was working for the Metro-slash-Lifestyle section of the paper. But *a Valentine piece?* It was insulting.

His coworkers—mostly fresh-faced, starry-eyed kids just out of college and far too sure of themselves— viewed him as something of an anomaly. He was nearly ten years older than many of them and the idea that at this point in his career he would take such a huge step backward by accepting a staff reporter's position in the Metro division was just plain weird in their books. But Jud had learned some hard but valuable lessons in pursuit of his career. The hardest had been when he'd been fired from a top paper in Virginia after he'd obtained information from a source he'd trusted. From Charlotte, a woman he'd thought was his friend…and more. Friendship had turned to romance shortly before he'd start to investigate Charles Blackwell. In fact, Charlotte had been the one to suggest he take a long hard look at Blackwell and his business dealings. She'd been so eager to help. Too eager. In hindsight he saw that she had been the driving force, assuring him that the documents she claimed to have were the real deal. He'd trusted her based on their long history as colleagues and based on the fact that he thought he might be falling in love with her, thought he knew her better than anyone. The information had turned out to be false and the paper had fired him. Needless to say, the romance ended at the same time.

He still remembered that last meeting with his editor. "You're good, Jud, but you're cocky. You've always been too focused on what a story can do for you and your career and in this business that almost always spells disaster."

Jud had bristled at the criticism. After all, he was hardly alone in being taken in by Charlotte's phony evidence. Everyone at the paper had agreed that this time, they had what they needed. Even the old man himself had been pushing the deadline.

"If you're willing to take a step back and work with one of the best, the managing editor at Washington Today is a friend and she's got an opening. I can get you in the door. After that...."

Washington Today was *the* alternative newspaper inside the beltway and it was beginning to gain national respect as well. When Millie had pointed out that she'd be taking a risk by hiring him, Jud had told her that he would accept any assignment. She had smiled and offered him the junior reporting position on the Metro beat. Metro included the softer Lifestyle features that even a paper like *Washington Today* understood the importance of offering to its readers. He could see that she was testing him, expecting him to turn it down. Instead, he swallowed what was left of his pride and accepted the job.

Jud was determined to prove himself by filing stories with unique angles and the kind of edgy inside-Washington slant that Millie loved. He wasn't interested in pleasing anyone but her, for she held the power to move him out of soft news and back into the hard, front-page stuff he longed to write. If he played this right, there was no telling where he might go.

Instead of taking the Metro, Grace walked from the Capitol to the Church on the Circle. She needed to think. She needed to discuss with God what had just happened. She probably needed to have her head examined.

"Okay, but You put us there at the same time," she muttered as if making her point to an unseen companion. "I mean, what were the possibilities that I would go there and meet this specific reporter? Not just any reporter, mind You, but one who has questionable ethics when it comes to getting a story."

She trudged on, oblivious to the curious stares of passersby, her cloche pulled low and her oversize prescription sunglasses blocking the glare of the January sun.

"I admit that the program could use some help, mostly in the form of more male participants. But why send him to spread the good news?" She almost stopped in her tracks. "Please tell me that You aren't thinking that Jud Marlowe is a good candidate for the program."

The thought immediately brought the clear image of Jud to mind. He was attractive in a sort of offbeat way. Good body. Obviously worked out. But he had this face that was practically etched with cynicism. In a novel, it would have been described as rugged. In reality, those features inspired curiosity and the need to know more. His eyes under the arch of brows that matched his cropped charcoal hair gave him a decidedly unapproachable look, except when he smiled. His smile changed everything. She'd noticed that immediately. Even when she was sizing him up as a potential problem for her father, the moment he smiled at her, something inside her had shifted.

"No. Jud has no need of a matchmaking program when he can turn that smile on and off to his advantage. So, what was it? Why did You choose him?"

She had no idea. She just knew that there was a reason Jud had been there at that moment, why she had been there to distract him from her father, and why she—against everything she normally did—had invited him to write a story on the program.

"So if we're going to play this thing out, the first thing I need to do is contact everyone in the program and let them know a reporter is going to be there so they can stay away if they like," she said and quickened her step, glad to have settled on a plan of action.

"Mom, it's Washington D.C., not Sodom and Gomorrah." On Tuesday evening, Jud cradled the cordless phone against one shoulder as he rescued a frozen pizza from his unpredictable oven. "Oh, great," he muttered softly under his breath as he deposited the burnt-edged, frozen-center pizza on the counter.

"Pay attention, young man," his mother ordered sternly before picking up the thread of the conversation he was desperately trying to end. "A nice girl is all I'm saying. How are you going to meet a nice girl in a place like Washington? Have you read the papers? This latest scandal...."

"Mom, I write for the papers, remember? Now tell me how to salvage a pizza that's both burnt and raw."

"Order in," she replied matter-of-factly. "We're not done with this, Jud Marlowe. You are thirty years old and more to the point, your father and I are nearly sixty. I want more than just to cradle your future children. I plan to see them graduate and get married themselves. This is your life. Get on with it."

"Working on it, Mom," Jud replied absently as he tried to locate the number of the pizza delivery place. "Put Dad on for a minute."

"Here, see if you can talk some sense into him," Jud heard his mother say as she passed his father the phone.

"How's the job?"

Good ol' Dad. Jud smiled. "It's okay," he replied.

When Jud had been fired, his parents had been there for him. The night he called to tell them what had happened, he'd begun with, "I messed up," and then given them the bare bones of the situation. They had listened and then his father had said, "There are no mistakes in life, son, only lessons to be learned."

At the time Jud had thought his father was naive, but

over the weeks that followed, he began to understand that he had indeed learned a valuable lesson. These days he was almost obsessive about personally checking every fact and every source before turning his stories over to the staff fact checkers at the paper. Even applying such standards to the no-brainer assignments Millie had been feeding him, he knew he was better for having perfected the practice.

Jud and his dad talked for a few minutes about his work, his dad's work, and people in the small Virginia town where he'd grown up. Then his father's voice dropped to almost a whisper.

"Your sisters are determined to surprise Mom for her sixtieth birthday. They've hired a band and everything. I think they've invited everyone we know and then some. Jenny wanted me to be sure to tell you to mark it on your calendar and to plan on bringing a date. You have to keep it quiet."

"What are you two whispering about?" Jud heard his Mom say and then his dad cleared his throat.

"Got it," Jud said. "Tell Jenny that I don't need her to organize my social life—I've got Mom for that."

His dad laughed, then said in a tone that was obviously for his wife's benefit, "Well, Jud, hang in there. I know it's frustrating not getting to go straight to the big stories, but you show them your stuff and you'll get there."

"I'll call you this weekend. Love to Mom," Jud added and hung up. He stared at the pizza. Suddenly eating alone was the last thing he wanted to do. Maybe they would serve something at the church. Either way, if he waited for that pizza to revive itself or for delivery, he'd be late. He grabbed his house keys and headed out.

It was warm for January. He replayed the phone call with his parents as he walked toward Dupont Circle. The details rarely changed. His mother wanted him to find a nice girl and get married and have a house full of children. If she knew he was on his way to a meeting with an honest-to-goodness matchmaker, she'd be thrilled. She had always seen his relationship with Charlotte for the convenience it was. She'd tried to warn him. And because her instincts had been right then, she seemed determined to take a personal interest in helping him find true romance. She had abandoned the subtle approach and he was going to have to be careful not to say too much about this particular assignment. Knowing his mom, she'd probably call Grace directly and suggest some ideas for matching him up with somebody.

Jud wanted somebody that he could engage in an intelligent conversation, who didn't roll her eyes at the idea of a thirty-mile bike ride and didn't get all hung up about protocol when it came to saying good-night. For reasons he couldn't fathom, he wondered how Grace Harrison would measure up in terms of those attributes.

She got points for being intelligent, but he doubted that she could survive the bike ride without whining. Good-night kiss protocol? Please! The woman didn't get his jokes. How on earth would she read his moves in the romance department? Not that he was interested. She was definitely not his type. He went in more for the blond outdoorsy sort—tall and tan with a flowing mane of hair—like Charlotte.

Jud forced himself to put aside any reminders of the woman who had claimed to love him and then thought nothing of trashing his career. He turned his attention back to Grace.

In the week since meeting her at the Capitol reception, he'd done extensive homework. Grace was the only daughter of Senator Riley Harrison, a popular Washington insider who had used his power to do some good things. She had practically turned steering clear of the political spotlight into an art. The "coffeehouse" was a gathering place located in the basement of a church in the Dupont Circle area of the city. From this base, the church offered a full program of activities aimed at attracting the young professional crowd to the church.

Talk about marketing religion, he thought sarcastically.

Since he'd begun doing background for the feature, Jud had interviewed the minister of the church. Reverend Timothy Gibbs was a fatherly sort and, not unexpectedly, he had sung Grace's praises long and loud. He had also suggested more than once that Jud might wish to attend services, strictly to gather information for his article, of course.

Jud saw through the ploy to get him back to church.

He also realized that the minister knew that he saw through it. Jud liked the older man for that. A minister with a sense of humor.

It had also surprised Jud to find half a dozen others who either had tried Grace's service or knew someone who had. According to one of her fans who happened to work at the paper, Grace's mission in life was to build strong Christian families and she was convinced the way to start was to make connections among the faithful. Please! He'd give away a week's pay to anyone who could prove that the statistics for so-called faith-based matches were any more successful than they were for the rest of the population.

He had actually jotted that down as one possible angle for the story. Looking for the downside of any story was a tough habit to break. But in reality, his mind kept going back to that reception. Why had Grace agreed to let him pursue a story that had to feature her in some way? What bigger story was she covering up by offering this tidbit? His plan was to gather background for the story on the program while getting a better read on Grace Harrison.

Chapter Three

Grace checked her watch and then the door three times in fifteen minutes.

"What is your problem?" Bethany asked as she set up the coffee supplies.

"I don't have a problem," Grace replied, glancing toward the door as it opened to admit three of the candidates for the evening's meeting.

"Coulda fooled me."

Grace recognized the sarcasm of that statement. She hadn't been able to fool her best friend since they started kindergarten together.

"It's that reporter, isn't it?" Bethany said as if she'd suddenly had an epiphany.

Grace frowned. "I don't know what I was thinking. To have allowed *any* reporter to do a story would have been a stretch, but this one?" She sat dejectedly on one of the high stools next to the counter. "What was I thinking?"

"Give the guy a chance, Gracie. Maybe he's really trying to redeem himself. How cool would that be?" She mimed reading a headline. "Matchmaker Expands to Redeeming Lost Souls."

"Maybe he won't come," Grace said.

"He'll come," Bethany replied with assurance. "It's meant to be—the whole business. You at the Capitol, when ordinarily you wouldn't go near the place. Him on the hunt for something that can turn his career, not to mention his life around...."

Grace couldn't help laughing. Bethany could be so dramatic but in such a good way. "You should write novels."

"And you should relax. This is your turf. He's the one who should be nervous."

Not likely, Grace thought. Jud didn't strike her as the kind of man who ever got nervous. She wondered how he had reacted the day he'd been called into his editor's office and fired. Her heart went out to him as she imagined the scene.

On the other hand, he had definitely landed on his feet. Most reporters could have kissed their career goodbye after a mistake like the one he'd made. He'd gotten a second chance. She hoped he appreciated it.

She had just given into the urge to check her watch and the door once more.

Aren't you better off if he doesn't come? If he decides to take a different direction with his story? But what if he's out there digging up stuff on me right now from unnamed sources?

You can't control everything, Grace.

"At the moment, I'd just like to control this," she muttered and resolutely refused to look at either her watch or the door.

Jud stood across the street from the Church on the Circle, watching people head for the side door with the awning that read *Coffeehouse—All Are Welcome.* Pretty classy entrance for a basement meeting space. He wondered if David had gotten there yet. He still had reservations about pretty much promising David that he wouldn't go after Grace. It wasn't as if he was looking to deliberately do an exposé on her or her father. Just because every instinct he had told him that something was in the works or Grace wouldn't have been at that reception. Just because every nerve ending in his body went on high alert at the very possibility of any story on the Harrisons did not mean that he would go to any lengths.

Dave would understand. In the end, he'd realize that Grace and her little matchmaking program could be Jud's best opportunity to get back in the big leagues.

After returning from the Capitol reception, he'd decided that for the time being it was important not to reveal his meeting with Grace to anyone else. He'd been able to evade Millie's questions by claiming to have a couple of angles he wanted to develop. But she was pushing him for details, mostly because she needed him to coordinate his idea with the art department so they could get going on photos or graphics as appropriate.

He wasn't ready to let Millie know that the real story was in the answers to questions like why Grace had been at the Capitol that day. Why her father must have needed her there. Why she had broken every rule the press knew she had and introduced herself to him—a reporter. He just hoped that when he gave Millie the David/Suni angle, the ambassador's name would be big enough to satisfy her. Jud had no doubt that if she knew what he was really going after, she'd give the lead to someone else. Millie was still a long way from entrusting a story on someone as powerful as Riley Harrison to Jud.

Taking the sign at its word that the place would even welcome those who had lapsed in the faith department, he dodged traffic on the Circle and headed for the entrance. He could hear the buzz of conversation as soon as he opened the heavy wooden door. Inside he followed the sound down a short flight of stairs and into a large social hall that had been converted into a surprisingly fashionable café. The gleaming copper cappuccino machines behind the long cherrywood counter would have been the pride of any trendy coffee franchise in the city.

A few couples sat at French-style café tables talking intently to each other. Jud immediately caught the aura of nervous tension that permeated the room. There were several empty tables. There were also about twice as many women as men. Jud smiled. Obviously, the program could use a little publicity. He stood in the shadows near the entrance and scanned the room.

David and Suni were working a table that featured literature, T-shirts and other propaganda designed to promote and raise money for the church. David waved, pointing Jud out to Suni, who smiled shyly in his direction. Jud wondered if this counted as a chaperoned date. Poor Dave, he thought.

"So, you found us, I see."

He hadn't heard Grace approach. "Hello again," he replied. "I decided to take you up on your invitation. Thought I'd see what it was all about."

"Did you get some coffee?" she asked and he noticed that she was wearing an ankle-length skirt in denim— along with a peach turtleneck that was only a minor improvement on the drab garb she'd worn at the Capitol function. She was also wearing her running shoes, which he found surprisingly charming.

"Oh, you serve coffee?" Again she gave him that blank look. "It's a joke," he said. "Coffeehouse—no coffee?"

"Got it," she said.

Grace led the way to the counter where the redhead that he'd seen at the reception was busy filling orders. "Hey, Bethany. New customer for you." She turned back to Jud and made the introductions. "Bethany Taft, Jud Marlowe. Jud's the reporter I was telling you about." She turned her attention to Jud. "Bethany is the church administrator and helps out here on Tuesday nights. She's distantly related to former President Taft."

"But I won't bore you with all the 'begats,'" Bethany said, topping off a mug with whipped cream from a spray can.

"Baguettes?" Jud wasn't sure of the connection between a French roll and being related to a nineteenth century president. On the other hand, he hadn't had supper—a baguette might....

Both Bethany and Grace laughed. "Not baguettes," Bethany said. "*Begats* as in the Bible. You know Adam begat Cain and Abel who begat the next generation who begat the next and so on."

"Cute," Jud said. *Somebody, help! I've walked into a den of religious fervor and I can't get out!*

"Now who's not getting the jokes?" Grace said with a smile as she put down her tea. "Bethany will take your order. We have coffee or tea. I'll be back in a few minutes."

He nodded and she was gone with a little wave of her hand. She moved with a confident athletic stride toward one of the tables on the other side of the room.

"What's your pleasure?"

Jud turned his attention to Bethany. She was tall and angular with straight hair that she twisted up in a haphazard way. She was wearing jeans and a fitted T-shirt with a coffee-stained apron tied low on her hips. She seemed right at home juggling the complex orders for coffee drinks. Jud pulled out his wallet. "Colombian. Black. Thanks."

"On the house tonight, at least the plain stuff. Now if you wanted a double mocha latte grande, that would cost you." Bethany grinned and presented the coffee in a heavy ceramic mug that read *God was on a deadline—that's why He took time to create caffeine.*

Jud surveyed the room and tried not to dwell on the fact that Bethany was entirely his type in the looks department and yet he felt no interest. Too much makeup, he decided. "Thanks," he said as he took a swallow of his coffee and turned so he could observe what was happening. Couples occupied several of the small tables. The extra females were sipping their lattes at the counter and sizing him up. He smiled briefly in their direction and turned his attention back to the couples at the tables.

In every case the man and woman involved were either leaning toward each other talking or listening intently. "So, how does this thing work?" Jud asked Bethany, who was polishing some freshly washed glass mugs and seemed inclined to play the role of the old-time bartender.

"They're all on a date," she replied nodding at the couples chattering away. "A ten-minute date."

"One of those speed dates," Jud said knowingly.

"Sort of. Watch." Bethany said.

Just then Grace rang a little bell and the room went silent as if someone had turned off the conversation like a faucet. Everyone gave Grace his or her attention. Jud couldn't help noticing that she was far less guarded and more at ease in this environment than she'd appeared at the Capitol function. Of course, this was her turf—not Daddy's. "Okay, how did that go?" she asked.

General noncommittal murmurs swept the room.

"That good, huh?" Grace ad-libbed with a grin. Everyone laughed and glanced nervously at the person sitting across the table.

So, she has a sense of humor after all. She just doesn't get *my* jokes.

"Take a moment," Grace continued. "Complete the card on your table and give it to me. Move around and stretch your legs. Get a refill. Next date starts in five minutes. Remember, gentlemen, move clockwise to the next table." She stepped away from the microphone and the chatter resumed, quieter now, more sporadic as the participants completed a small card—green for the men and yellow for the women. Grace moved through the room collecting them.

Jud turned back to Bethany. "So, tell me about Grace's version of speed dating."

Bethany splashed coffee into Jud's half-empty mug. "Each man meets each woman for ten minutes. The ladies stay at the same table throughout the evening. The guys move in a clockwise direction."

"And the benchwarmers?" He cocked his head in the general direction of the women waiting at the coffee counter.

Bethany laughed. "They'll get their turn."

Grace joined him at the coffee counter where Bethany handed her a steaming mug of tea. "I can imagine that this must look like some kind of weird ritual," she said with a genuine laugh that had a captivating way of bubbling up from somewhere deep inside of her. It made her even more of the gamine than he'd first thought. Audrey Hepburn came to mind. The fact that his mother really liked Audrey Hepburn also came to mind.

Jud switched his coffee to his left hand so he could fish his handheld tape recorder out of his right jacket pocket. The mug tipped and he felt the hot liquid spill across his hand.

Grace and Bethany grabbed a bunch of napkins and began sopping up the coffee from his hand and the counter. The benchwarmers made clucking sounds of concern. "You okay?" Grace asked.

Somehow he found his sense of humor in spite of the scalding coffee. "I'm pretty sure clumsiness isn't terminal," he replied. She didn't seem convinced. "I'm fine," he assured her.

"Well, if you're sure," she said not looking at all convinced, "okay, then, let me explain how this works."

He laid the tape machine between them, pressing the record button. He waited while Bethany poured him a fresh cup of coffee. Grace reached over and switched off the recorder. "I'd rather not have this so obvious. Let's let them get through a few rounds and then I'll remind them that you're here."

Jud frowned, but put the recorder away. "They already know about me? About the story?"

"Of course. I told you that I was concerned about confidentiality so we called everyone and let them know that a reporter might attend tonight's session. That way they could elect not to come."

"And did anyone 'elect not to come'?"

She shrugged. "A few, but you have a very nice mixture of backgrounds and personalities here. I think you'll be able to gather a couple of interesting comments."

"Okay. So, give me the overview."

"Everyone is here to meet someone—" she began warming her hands on her own mug "—hopefully *the* someone, but barring that at least someone they can see spending more time with in the weeks to come."

"Where did they come from?" These losers who need you to find them a date in a city that is literally teeming with beautiful intelligent young single people.

She shrugged. "Most live in the area. Word spreads and sometimes we get people from other areas of the city."

"Why here? Why a church social hall?"

"Aside from the program's commitment to faith-based relationships, it's neutral territory and safe. Respectable. In the beginning there's a group aspect to the process to put people more at ease."

"They just show up? No screening?"

"Of course, we pre-screen. Everyone registers and completes a fairly comprehensive bio. If they seem right for the program, then Bethany or I interview them in person."

"Sounds like it might be easier getting into Harvard," he said in an attempt to take some of the edge off her defensiveness.

She sipped her tea. "When you offer a service like this, people appreciate it when you take extra care. Those in the program have been promised a sincere commitment that all participants are serious about their faith and about the idea of finding a lasting relationship."

"What does it cost?" Jud asked.

"It's free—part of the church's adult education program." She set the mug down. "Excuse me for just a minute."

Jud watched her walk among the tables, visiting with people along the way. When Grace reached the front of the room, she rang the small silver bell again. Everyone took an empty chair and faced a new partner. "And begin by just saying hello," she said softly to the group, striking the bell a second time.

The chatter began, hesitant at first and then more freely. A laugh here. An exclamation of surprise somewhere else.

"So anyway, people sign up to come and meet other people of like interests." She was back taking up the conversation where she'd left off.

"Like interests?"

"Their faith. Her expression left no doubt that she was beginning to see him as a slow learner in need of a constant reminder when it came to this fact. "As I mentioned, it's extremely hard for busy professional people to meet someone. That probably triples when it comes to meeting someone who has the same commitment to faith."

A look must have crossed his face because she paused and then said, "What?"

No sense beating around the bush. "I haven't done the research yet, but what if I find out that there's no difference between success rates for couples who start out with this commitment to faith and those who have other things in common that make them compatible."

She looked at him as if he had just arrived from Mars. "It's not just a question of compatibility," she explained and her tone made it clear that this ought to be obvious. "It's really hard to get to know somebody, even start to build a relationship and then find out that you've been on different paths all along. In this day and age we need to do everything we can to help people of strong faith find each other from the outset." Her eyes gleamed with the fire of her convictions.

"Are there so few of you true believers left?" he couldn't resist asking.

"Ho, boy," he heard Bethany mutter under her breath as she turned to fill an order from a benchwarmer.

Grace's eyes widened and her full mouth thinned before she took a deep breath and carefully arranged her expression to one of polite consideration of the question.

"My mistake. When we spoke at the Capitol last week, I understood you to indicate that you were one of 'us.' I believe you called it giving me your 'credentials'?"

"Refill?" Bethany said, and Grace waved her away, her eyes never leaving Jud's face.

"I…"

"Let's see," she continued as if he had not spoken. "Church services in your mother's arms as an infant, Sunday school, choir, youth leader, camp, church college." She ticked each off on her manicured fingers. "Am I missing anything?" she asked sweetly and before he could answer, added, "Ah, yes. I should have noticed that the litany stops at college."

"Okay, point taken. Look, I'm a journalist. It's my job to look for the opposing side to a story."

Grace leaned a fraction of an inch closer and her voice was low. "Point taken, but it is possible to accomplish that without deception or trickery."

Jud felt his own defenses rise. "All of that was true."

"No doubt. But what about after college? Where has your faith taken you recently?"

She was very good at interviewing him. She had managed to take complete control of the direction of the conversation. Jud summoned a smile.

Since the smile wasn't working, he cleared his throat, dropped any attempt at charming her and said, "I apologize," and meant it.

The tightness around Grace's mouth lessened a fraction. She didn't say anything but her eyes invited him to continue.

"I was trying to impress you at the Capitol and that crack just now about so few true believers being left was way out of line."

She stared at him through the wire rim glasses for a long moment, then nodded once and sat up straight again. "Getting back to the program," she said firmly, "let's take Suni and David, for example."

"What about them?" Jud asked, relieved to be back on topic.

"Her father is a member of the diplomatic community and he wants the best for Suni. For now that means having her settle here in America, and for the ambassador, that means having her married. He suggested that Suni participate in this program because he saw an element of security when screening appropriate candidates for her."

"Sounds like a recipe for conflict. I mean Suni must have her own ideas about dating and choosing a husband."

"Exactly," Grace agreed. "But because Suni's family will soon be going back to a place that Suni really has never thought of as home, her parents are doing everything they can to help her stay. On the other hand, her father does have some old-fashioned values and they don't include Suni living on her own in Washington."

"She's a grown woman and more American than Sri Lankan. Why not trust her to find her own way?"

"That's where this program comes in." Grace grinned. "Suni came to me for help—we've been friends for years and our parents are also good friends. Anyway, her father agreed that if she followed the program and she found a proper husband, then he would accept that and she could stay. Enter David Forrester, who had joined the program about a month earlier and really hadn't had much success finding a match."

He'd had no idea that David had been attending these sessions for so long. One day he'd started talking about Suni and it was as if she'd dropped into his life out of the blue.

"But then apparently you already know David or were you looking for another story when you spoke with him at such length at the reception?"

Her tone had changed. It was polite, but there was no warmth to it.

"We're old friends," Jud admitted.

Grace frowned. "Then no doubt you already knew about Suni's background and their romance." She sighed. "Just when I decide that this story might be a good idea, you do or say something that makes me wonder. I don't appreciate having people waste my time, Mr. Marlowe."

"Round Two," Jud heard Bethany mutter.

"Look," Jud replied, chuckling in an attempt to disarm her, "you started telling the story. I wanted to hear your version of it. That's all."

The frown didn't disappear. "There are no *versions* to anything that happens here or that I tell you."

"Okay. Poor choice of words. I just meant…"

"And another thing," Grace said, warming to the challenge.

Bethany picked up the small silver bell that Grace had left on the counter and rang it. "Round Three," she said.

Grace and Jud looked up at the sound of the bell, as did everyone else in the room. Bethany grinned and nodded toward the clock, then said softly so that only Grace and Jud heard her, "Did I say *Round Three?* I got confused. For a minute there I thought I was back in the days of the old Friday night fights." She flashed an innocent smile and handed the bell to Grace. "Time to switch tables again."

When Grace left, Bethany leaned across the counter.

"You're going to want to play things really straight with Gracie," she said. "If you're interested, that is, and it would appear that you are."

"Not in the way you mean it. I'm just getting background for my story."

"Uh-huh," Bethany replied. "And I'm just offering a little friendly advice." Then she capped off two coffee drinks with chocolate shavings and called, "Order up!"

Grace used this break to explain Jud's presence. She reminded everyone of her call earlier that week. She made a small joke about how the number of men and women was off because a couple of people had declined to come to another session.

"Apparently the women are braver than the men in this case," Grace said and everyone laughed.

She went on to offer the opportunity for anyone who didn't like the idea of being part of a story to decline Jud's request for an interview. She passed out a lavender card, made a joke about purple prose and asked each person to indicate his or her willingness to be part of the story in terms of being interviewed, quoted and perhaps photographed. Jud couldn't help but be impressed with the way she was covering herself, the program and the church from all angles, and yet, it didn't come across as self-serving. It sounded as if she was genuinely concerned that the participants not have their privacy invaded by the press.

She took her time before coming back to the counter. When she finally took the stool next to his, she was composed and ready to continue the interview. "Where were we?" she asked sorting through the green and yellow matchmaker cards she'd collected from the previous round.

"Tell me more about how the ten-minute date works."

While she might have gotten control of her irritation when speaking to the participants, her tone with him was still cool. It was the kind of polite but distant tone that he assumed she employed for any interview.

"They share all that normal first date kind of information. Where are you from, what do you do, where did you go to school—that sort of introductory getting-to-know-you stuff. Mostly, we attract people who have moved to D.C. from other places. They see a lot of people in their jobs, especially those that work in the government. But a job isn't a life. Things can get pretty lonely." She stared at him for a moment and added, "Even for people like you, I would assume."

Jud wasn't about to admit to a professional matchmaker that he'd been scammed by a woman he'd been convinced was in love with him. On the other hand, since cutting his losses with Charlotte and moving to D.C., he couldn't deny that there had been times when he spent an inordinate amount of time channel surfing with no real interest in watching anything on TV. He also had to admit that in spite of family close by and a host of friends, there were times when he wished there were someone—female—that he could just hang out with and talk to about anything and everything. He sometimes wished he was in the kind of relationship that had moved beyond protocol to just *being*.

She sighed. "But I digress. Where was I?"

Jud realized that she'd gone on talking and he hadn't been listening. "What happens after ten minutes?" he reminded her.

"At the end, they complete one question on the card. Would you like to see this person again? If the answer from both parties is yes, then in the coming week we move on to the next step."

"And if one person says no?"

Grace shrugged. "That's life. Chances are that in meeting different people tonight everyone here will have at least one mutual yes. Most will have two or three. That's pretty good odds when you're single and alone in a city like this."

Jud couldn't argue the point. Still there was the question of what she got out of this. "Is that how you met your true love?" he asked, and this time his attempt at charm seemed to work.

"Off-limits," she replied, shaking her finger sternly at him, but with a smile.

He laughed. "You sure do have a lot of ground rules about what's on and off the record," he teased.

"I'm the facilitator of the program here at the Church on the Circle. Even if I were in the market to meet someone…"

"Which she's not, but should be," Bethany interjected as she passed them on her way to help deliver mugs of coffee.

"Which I'm not," Grace repeated for Bethany's benefit. "But even if I were, using the program would be a conflict of interest."

"This is a paid position then?" It was unexpected information. "I thought you were a volunteer."

"I'm the director of adult programming and education. This is one of the free programs we offer."

He took a moment to digest this latest bit of news. There had been little detail about her work at the church in the background work he'd done. Where it did come up, the research made it sound as if it was some kind of charity work she did, not a full-time job. He stored this revelation with the other information he'd discovered.

This whole matchmaker thing was beginning to have all the ingredients to be exactly what Millie wanted for Valentine's Day. Maybe he could risk telling her that he'd met Grace Harrison after all.

"What? Did you picture me sitting around eating chicken salad lunches at charity gigs?"

He felt a flush of color along his collar line and grinned. "Maybe not the chicken salad lunch," he admitted, "more like attending board meetings."

She laughed and this time it was genuine.

"So, what about you, Jud Marlowe?" she asked, indicating an empty table on the edge of the circle of occupied tables. "Want to give it a shot?"

"I thought I needed to be pre-screened."

"Ah, but in your case, this is all just research, isn't it? So the order of things really isn't an issue."

Before he could refuse, Grace led the way to the table. "You might as well get your feet wet." She glanced around the room. "I'll make it easier on you. I'll be your first date." She sat across from him, rang the small silver bell and a new session began. "So, Jud, what brought you to D.C.?"

Chapter Four

Grace was relieved and a little surprised to see that in the next ten minutes Jud fell easily into the rhythm of the process. He talked about his job at the newspaper—blowing off his current position as nothing more than a temporary stop on his way to meatier assignments. He told her about growing up in Virginia, close enough to Washington that it always felt like home. He even told her about his mother and how she was driving him crazy to find a wife. Grace suppressed a smile. She was positive that even he could not believe the things coming out of his mouth. And all she had to do was listen—both for what he said and what he left out. He didn't talk at all about past relationships.

"And, I like to work out," he said, then paused apparently considering what he might have forgotten to mention.

"Where do you work out?"

"The YMCA over on K Street."

She mentally ran through the regulars who exercised around the same time she did. "I work out there regularly. I don't remember seeing you," she said.

"I work pretty odd hours so I'm usually there when the place is pretty dead."

"Wait. You do the bike and keep a towel over your head, right?"

He smiled. "Guilty."

"I have seen you—but I didn't know it. I do that sometimes, too. Go at off hours. People are usually nice about not bothering me. Heaven knows I'm hardly a famous person, but it's a popular place for Washington celebrities, mostly because the management maintains a strict policy of privacy."

Grace paused. She had learned the trick of leaving silences in need of filling from her father. It was also a reporter's trick, and she took some pleasure in turning it on him.

"So, tell me about you," he said when the silence threatened to become awkward.

"We have a lot in common," she said. "I grew up in the heart of Washington and love everything it stands for. My parents, for all their fame, are quite ordinary people. Mom attended all the parent-teacher things at school and Dad was always there for the special programs and open houses. I got my undergrad and master's degrees at Georgetown in clinical psychology."

"And, of course, that led straight to a career as a matchmaker," he teased.

She smiled. "Once I realized my true calling, I went

for a second graduate degree in religious education and church administration."

"And the matchmaking?"

She shrugged. "It's just something I fell into. I helped a couple of friends, and then a couple of members of the congregation got together with my help. From there it just kind of happened." She glanced at her watch. "Oops. We've run long."

She reached across the table and laid her hand on his. "So, how about trying this for real?" When he hesitated, she added, "I mean with an actual candidate. It'll be the best way to meet the others and decide who might be a good interview—at least among the women."

"Okay if I take notes now that everyone's been properly warned…twice?" he asked, taking out the recorder again.

"Fine." Grace turned and glanced around the room. "That's Elaine Bennett," she said pointing to a tall blonde sitting at the counter. "She's very outgoing and probably a great interview. Why don't you start with her? I think the two of you might really hit it off."

Then Grace tapped the bell to indicate yet another shift in the dance of ten-minute dating. This time she pointed out to the others that Jud was trying out the program. She motioned to Elaine, inviting her to take the chair opposite Jud. Jud stood politely and waited while Elaine sat down.

For the next ten minutes, Grace sat at the counter and watched Jud with Elaine. He was different than he'd been with her—bolder and more relaxed. He talked, but so did Elaine. Well, of course, silly. He's asking her questions; she's answering. It's called an interview.

Jud leaned toward Elaine, his expression serious as he listened intently. Was he actually flirting? So, what if he was? The important thing was that they really seemed to hit it off.

"Earth to Gracie," Bethany murmured, her eyes also on Jud and Elaine. "A perfect match?"

"Perhaps. Although he insists that he's simply here to do research for his article."

"How's *your* research coming?"

"Stop matchmaking," Grace said, turning her back on Jud and Elaine.

Bethany feigned shock. "Man, I thought that's why we were here."

"I'm going to talk to David. I need to know if Jud can be trusted," Grace said. She rang the bell and polished off the last of her tea, then leaned over the counter to deposit her mug with the rest of the dirty dishes.

"Like Dave would rat out a friend," Bethany said. "What do you expect him to say? 'Stay away from my buddy. He's no good.'"

"David will tell me the truth, which I suspect is that Jud is a terrific and loyal friend, but when it comes to his work, he operates on a different playing field. Besides, if Dave won't level with me, Suni will."

"What is it about this guy that has you so hyper?"

"I'm not hyper. I'm just being cautious."

"Whatever you say, but at the moment you might want to rethink asking Dave what he thinks of Jud, since Jud is already over there talking to him and Suni."

Sure enough, instead of moving to the next table in the circle, Jud was at the literature table, browsing the contents as he said something that made David and Suni laugh.

"He's a reporter, Gracie," Bethany reminded her. "You really have no control over how he goes about getting his story."

"I don't completely trust him."

"Then ask yourself why he's here?" Bethany raised her eyebrows. "I know I didn't invite him."

Grace opened her mouth to reply but then closed it. Bethany had a point.

"Well, what do you think?" David asked Jud.

"Frankly, I don't get it. I mean this woman," he said motioning toward Elaine, "is terrific. She should be fighting guys off with a stick. What is she doing here?"

"Did you ask her?" Suni asked.

"I did. She gave me this line about how important it is at this stage of her life to not waste time going out with men who don't share her religious beliefs or dedication."

"Makes sense to me," David said.

"But it limits the playing field," Jud protested.

Suni smiled and handed him a pamphlet that described the program. "That's the point. See? The program is for those who are ready to be serious about finding a partner. People who know what they want." She looked adoringly up at David. He squeezed her hand.

"Is that allowed?" Jud asked with a nod toward their entwined fingers.

David laughed. "Most definitely. And, as usual, you've changed the subject. It's a bad habit, Jud."

Suni gathered several pieces of literature and handed them to him. "I think perhaps these might help you in writing your article. Would you like to interview David and me separately, together or both?"

Jud had gotten so caught up in trying to settle on an angle tied to Grace that he'd almost forgotten the discussion with Dave about the story he wanted to do.

"Both," he replied with a grin. "How does tomorrow work for you, Suni? Breakfast? Coffee?"

"Can't. Could you come to the embassy for lunch?" she asked.

"It's a date," Jud said.

He took the pamphlets and turned to see Grace glance his way as she headed toward the front of the room, where she reminded everyone that this would be their last match-up of the evening.

"Any of you who would be willing for Mr. Marlowe to contact you for his article on the program, please take a moment now and place your completed card in the basket as Bethany passes among you."

A few people busied themselves with getting more coffee instead of completing the cards. But Jud was relieved to have two women and one man hand him their business cards without bothering with Grace's lavender form.

"Looks like I might have to rely on you for the male point of view," he said to David.

Grace rang the bell and prepared everyone for the evening's final session. Jud used the opportunity to say goodbye to David and Suni and leave his empty coffee mug with Bethany, who handed him three more lavender cards. He turned at the door, caught Grace's attention and waved. The look she gave him in return was very familiar to him—it was the look of someone who was having serious second thoughts about letting a reporter into her life.

Later, as Grace and Bethany closed up for the night, Grace couldn't seem to get Jud off of her mind.

"You do understand that I have quite possibly made an enormous mistake by letting him pursue this article?" she said as she turned chairs over and placed them on top of the tables.

"Why? Where's the harm?"

"How can you ask that?"

Bethany frowned. "It's not like you. You always see the best in a person. What is your problem with Jud?"

"He's a skeptic and a cynic, a borderline nonbeliever. Do you know that he actually wanted to know what I would say if he could produce statistics to show that there's no difference in success between faith-based and non-faith-based marriages?"

"And what did you say?"

"Nothing, but I should have said that anyone can take numbers and make them support a particular point of view. Just look at what they do with political polls."

"And just what would Jud's point of view be?"

Grace turned on the dishwasher under the counter and spoke over the noise. "If I had to guess, I'd say that he's one of those people who views anything based on religion with suspicion. Apparently somewhere after college graduation, the man misplaced everything his parents brought him up to believe about God and faith."

"A lapsed soul! Ah, maybe it's not the dating thing at all that God has in mind." Bethany took a stool from her and set it on the counter.

"You could be right," Grace replied.

"Of course, I am. I mean what were the chances the two of you would ever meet in this lifetime?"

Grace went on stacking chairs on top of tables. "What if he only *thinks* he came to get a story," Grace continued more to herself than her friend. "What if God led him here for some other reason? Of course then the question is 'Why?'"

"Maybe he's in need of a match with—for," Bethany said with a sly grin and turned her attention to polishing the copper coffee urns.

"Forget that. He's not at all a candidate for the program. He had the audacity to make one of his bad jokes about people of faith. You heard him." She didn't wait for a response. "And then there's the fact that he wasn't exactly up-front about knowing about David and Suni.

Plus he has yet to even mention his part in the whole Blackwell exposé."

"Hmmm. On the other hand, you're not exactly being straight with him about that, are you?"

"Okay. Good point."

"Maybe he thinks you don't know about that?"

Grace shrugged. "Who knows? He's sure not working overtime trying to impress me or at least reassure me."

"Could be he's moved on and figures you have as well. I mean it's been what—over a year? Besides, your dad was only mentioned in passing as part of a list of influential people that Charlie knew."

Grace considered this along with the fact that she had been overreacting ever since she'd first met Jud. "You may have a point."

Bethany grinned.

"But," Grace said in her firm schoolmarm voice, "let's get one thing straight. He's here to do a story. He'll be gone in a week or so. He is not a candidate for our program."

"But you've got to admit that he'd be a great addition," Bethany said. "I mean he's thirtysomething, a little world-weary and absolutely convinced that he needs no help in the relationship department."

Grace laughed. "Or God could just have sent him to tell our story. Let's go," she said. "It's late and we both have to work tomorrow."

"Well, at least we agree that God has a hand in this, Come on, I'll give you a lift," Bethany offered.

"Just to the Metro and then you need to get home and call Nick," Grace said as they walked to Bethany's car.

"Have I thanked you for forcing me to see that Nick was the right man for me? If you hadn't dumped him…"

"I didn't dump him."

"Pretty much. According to Nick, you even used the old 'I think we need to see other people' line."

Grace smiled sheepishly. "Well, the important thing is that it worked out."

"For me and Nick. The jury's still out on you. On the other hand, Jud has some potential."

"I thought *I* was the matchmaker," Grace replied.

"Well, then *physician, heal thyself,*" Bethany said.

"All kidding aside," Grace said as Bethany pulled up to the Metro station that would take Grace to her parents' home in Alexandria, "it would be great if Jud ended up rediscovering his faith in the process of doing this story."

"And it would also be terrific if my best friend would finally find a man worthy of her," Bethany said.

"There is no way that Jud is that man."

"Never say never."

"Never!" Grace shouted. "The last man I need in my life is a reporter. See you in church, Bethie." She kissed her friend on the cheek.

"See you in church, Gracie," Bethany replied and watched as Grace ran down the stairs to catch the next train.

Back in his apartment, Jud waited half an hour and then started calling the people who had given him their cards. Strike while the iron is hot, his former editor had always advised. He reached three of the four, and with tape machine rolling and the phone on speaker, he conducted his interviews.

Around midnight, he switched on the all-news channel for background and turned on his laptop. While he waited for it to load, he made a label with the topic, date and place of the interviews and placed it precisely on the cassette he'd recorded with Elaine and others at the church and later on the phone. He rewound the tape while he opened a blank document, then prepared to transcribe the interview with Elaine Bennett.

He leaned back and pictured her sitting across the table from him. After several years as a senior Congressional staffer, Elaine had taken a high-profile job as a lobbyist for the insurance industry. She admitted to being over thirty; to loving her work; to an affinity for shoes that took a chunk of every paycheck; and to being ready to settle down to marriage and a family.

Jud keyed the setting, the date and Elaine's full name and contact information onto the document and switched on the recorder.

JM: What's a terrific looking woman like you doing in a place like this?

EB: Did you get that line from your father or grandfather? (More serious.) All kidding aside, I think it's a wonderful idea to do a story about this program. People need to know that it's here.

JM: And that's because...?

EB: Meeting someone who might actually be a serious candidate—The one—in this city is... is...well, let's just say it's not easy.

JM: Okay, so it's a good place to meet guys. What else?

EB: Not just any guy, Jud. Think about how great it would be to have all the preliminaries out of the way.

JM: Such as?

EB: For me, it's vitally important that I marry someone who believes as I do, who will not only agree to raise our children in a religious home, but who will actively participate in that mission.

JM: Go on.

EB: When you meet someone the normal way there are two topics you tend to shy away from until you're more sure of the other person—religion and politics, especially religion. But for me and everyone here, Grace has helped us to see that our beliefs and faith are the foundation of how we do our jobs, how we choose our social activities, how we....

JM: Got it. So, how did Grace Harrison get into this business?

EB: No one here is going to help you dig up news on Grace, Jud.

JM: The article is on the program. Grace pioneered the program. I can't exactly keep her out of this.

EB: Look, time's almost up. Here's my card if you have more questions about the program and what it has meant to me. Grace is about to have us change tables, and frankly I've been wanting to meet the guy who's about to follow you—not that you aren't perfectly nice, but after all, Grace says you're not a candidate, right?

JM: Right.

End of interview. Jud sat staring at his notes for a long moment. Given Elaine's reaction to the mere mention of Gracc, he wondered if Grace made participants sign some sort of loyalty oath before joining the program.

In the background the news played on.

"Senator Gordon continues to deny that he's been in touch with the leadership of the opposition on more than one occasion. Is it possible that he could be pondering a potential change in party loyalty? In other news…"

Jud spun around to face the TV, his mind processing images that sprang to the forefront with the reporter's words. *Senator Gordon…leadership of the opposition…possible party switch.* Jud flashed back to the reception at the Capitol. He'd spotted Riley Harrison working the crowd, and then out of nowhere the reclusive Grace Harrison had approached Jud. He'd been looking toward her father. She had turned him around—away from what? Her father and who else?

Jud closed his eyes and focused on every detail of

that afternoon. When Grace walked away, she had started in one direction, toward Bethany. Then what?

Her father called out to her as he was shaking hands with Senator Mark Gordon.

Bingo, Jud thought. "Leadership of the party opposition" does not go much higher than Riley Harrison if you're Senator Gordon.

A slow grin spread across his face. He had the gift of an almost perfect photographic memory for details he had seen but failed to fully absorb. Now he recalled that when he was talking to David and watching Grace approach her father and Senator Gordon, it had taken some time for her to work her way through the crowd. People noticed her, stopped to greet her, were obviously surprised to see her.

What about the two senators?

They had waited, smiling and exchanging pleasantries.

Or might that have been a smoke screen? Why would the senator call attention to his daughter?

To buy time. Time that had given them the opportunity to exchange a lot more than simple polite chitchat. Two or three minutes—a lifetime in a political conversation.

His heart sank as he wondered how many other journalists had noticed the same sequence of events and put it together—how many of them hadn't been distracted by Grace? On the other hand, the event had attracted only the bottom-feeders like him. None of the big-name journalists had been there. So far there'd been nothing but the one item. It had to mean that if others had their suspicions, then they were working their sources for all they were worth before they broke a story.

The good news for him was that no one had his connection to the senator's daughter. If he handled this right and gained Grace's trust, then he'd have an inside track to her father.

Of course, he would need a lot more than just a replay of the events of that afternoon before he took this to Millie. He could almost see the editor's skeptical look if he told her that he had this hunch based on what he thought he'd seen, but nothing to back it up.

Oh, yeah, Marlowe. She'll buy that, based on your background for coming up with reliable information, she'll just be all over that.

He started checking blogger sites to see what the chatter was and what was being reported beyond this meeting at the reception. One site did note that the two senators had greeted each other at the reception but dismissed this as the usual photo op before the Congress got down to business. All other chatter focused on the newly elected members and how they might influence the coming session.

Who am I kidding? Millie's probably already got Grady Hunter working the story.

Still, he had his hunch and, despite his fiasco with the Blackwell story, his hunches could be trusted. He was in the race and Jud was confident about one thing— he knew what he'd seen. He knew that Grace had deliberately diverted his attention from her father. Then her father had used her to divert attention from himself and Gordon. And, best of all, he now had a possible explanation for why Grace had materialized out of nowhere that day.

Chapter Five

Grace was having a restless night and finally gave up trying to sleep. Allowing Jud into her life hadn't been her finest hour. She wavered between wanting him to do the story on the matchmaking program and figuring out the fastest way to extricate herself from the entire situation ASAP. She had no doubt that she was right, that his real interest had been in her father that day at the Capitol. She also suspected that he might have spotted her father and Senator Gordon together. Of course, her father thought they had pulled off that business about introducing her to the senator, but had it worked?

When she'd asked her dad why he'd take the risk of being seen publicly with Senator Gordon, he'd told her that Gordon was paranoid about phone calls and e-mails being traceable. It was Ken who had suggested the brief exchange in plain sight. No one would suspect that two seasoned veterans of the Senate would be so brazen. The staff had been there to make sure that no reporter was within listening distance of anything the two men might say. Had it worked?

Somehow she didn't think that Jud missed much and if he'd noticed the two senators... She should have put her father off and fought her way through the crowd to Bethany instead. That would have held Jud's attention. Bethany was the kind of woman every man looked at a second and even third time.

He's also a journalist.

Grace flipped on the news and caught the end of a piece speculating on Senator Gordon and his plans for the future now that the new Congress was in session. She flipped through all the channels hoping to get more details, and at the same time feeling a sense of relief when there was nothing more.

Sooner or later Jud was bound to realize how odd it was for her to be at the reception in the first place. What if he had also heard the reporter's comment about Senator Gordon? As an experienced if sullied journalist, he was bound to put the two facts together. And if he did, would he hope to use his connection to her to gather more information?

"Oh, yeah, like that's a huge mystery," she said aloud as she turned off the TV, flopped back on her bed and stared at the ceiling. "The man is after a story. Not only that, after the Blackwell fiasco, he's desperate to redeem his career. He's after the biggest scoop he can land."

In addition to her monologues with God, Grace frequently carried on dialogues with herself.

What did you expect?

She sighed. "Okay, well, I hoped he might be different."

Why?

"Because…."

Because?

"I give up." She threw back the covers in frustration and started practicing a couple of stretching moves hoping to relax and get some sleep.

Think, Grace.

"Okay. Why should I care one way or the other if Jud turns out to be just like any other journalist looking for his big break?"

Grace considered that as she switched positions. Then she froze, teetering on one leg, her arms stretched high.

"Got it," she said, sitting on the bed and grinning. "Bethany's right. Two can play at this game. If I can keep him occupied with the story of the program, then I can keep an eye on him. If he did notice anything and/or hear the rumors, I'll be able to warn Dad and Senator Gordon that he's getting too close. In the meantime, I'll counter by devoting my all to getting him back on track with the moral compass he seems to have lost."

She flopped back onto the bed, relaxed and feeling great.

Grace lay awake for another hour considering potential ways she might use this opportunity to help Jud and protect her father at the same time. Bethany suggested matching him up with someone in the program might be the answer. Of course.

Bethany also had the idea that the match ought to be with Grace.

She mentally ran through the women who had attended the session. Elaine was really the only possibility. She had a little bit of an edge to her and a very good sense of humor. Grace was sure that a sense of humor would be important in building a relationship with Jud.

The following morning Grace was so caught up in thinking about a plan of action which could bring Elaine and Jud together that she was halfway to work before she realized that she was wearing two different-colored socks. She sighed. For the daughter of one of Washington's most dapper senators, she was certainly fashion-challenged. Fortunately, the trousers of her wool pantsuit limited exposure of her mistake, but she knew that Bethany would be sure to notice it at some point.

"Call for you, Gracie," Kim Jenson the church secretary said as soon as Grace entered the office. "I put the name and number there in your mailbox."

"Thanks, Kim."

Grace checked the slip and ignored Bethany's grin.

"Somebody's not wasting any time," her best friend said.

"No doubt, he's on a deadline," Grace replied.

"Really? He told me this was a Valentine's Day story and that's still, let's see, several weeks away?"

"I'll be downstairs," Grace said as she left the office and read the note again.

Jud Marlowe from the meeting last night. 555-8576.

Grace found it touching the way he'd obviously felt the need to remind her of the connection between them. As if she wouldn't remember him.

"Kim took the message, probably added that herself," Grace muttered. But Kim rarely added anything to messages. She simply wrote down exactly what the other person said.

Taking off her coat, Grace quickly rifled through the rest of her mail and messages before turning to the phone. She didn't attempt to analyze the fact that she was uncommonly ambivalent about returning his call.

"What are you, in high school?" She entered the number from Kim's note.

A recorded voice informed her that Jud was unavailable at the moment and to leave a message or try later. Relieved, Grace hung up and turned to tackle the several projects awaiting her attention. Jud Marlowe was taking far too much of her time.

Jud stifled a yawn. Millie was really pouring it on. In the days since the reception, she'd handed him half a dozen additional assignments to cover. He faced three deadlines today alone. Not that he couldn't do every one of them in his sleep. This morning's assignment was to cover the meeting of the city's parks commission. The topic was beautification—not exactly his area of interest, but he forced himself to focus. He failed, of course.

Since his visit to the coffeehouse, he'd been working overtime to come up with various angles he might offer Millie on the story of Grace Harrison's dating game without revealing the Grace connection. After hearing the news item the night before, he was more determined than ever to find a potential link between Senators Harrison and Gordon. He couldn't lose this chance to revive his career.

What surprised Jud was that every time he thought about getting the scoop on the senator, he felt a deep-seated kernel of something that he could only describe as a foreboding. It was that same feeling he'd had before the bottom fell out of the Blackwell article. It's called self-doubt, he thought, but knew that wasn't all of it.

Or guilt?

What have I got to be guilty about? These are public servants and how they do their job is fair game.

Guilt because of Grace?

Now that's just reaching. I barely know her.

There's something about her though.

Jud forced his attention back to the business at hand. He wasn't about to ignore this inner dialogue with a voice that he identified as being sometimes his mother and sometimes just his conscience. However, he was going to keep it at bay while he dug deeper for the possibility that Harrison and Gordon were cooking up something. And anything two such powerful men collaborated on had the potential to affect the nation's future for years to come.

On the other hand, he couldn't deny that meeting Grace at the Capitol, followed by that evening at the coffeehouse, complicated matters. There was something about her, an instinct not to disappoint her—dangerous for a journalist out for any story, but career-ending for someone trying to redeem himself in an industry where usually it was one strike and you're out.

Focus, Marlowe! He turned his attention back to the report of the parks commissioner.

That lasted a good thirty seconds before he found himself staring at the cell phone he'd been asked to turn off during the meeting. He wondered if she'd gotten his message. He wondered if she'd tried to call. If she hadn't, how should he play this? If he appeared too eager, she'd get suspicious. After all, she was obviously incredibly bright and her experience living in the political limelight had to have taught her how to read certain signals. Better to play it cool.

"And with that, we're adjourned," he heard the chairperson announce. The cell phone was back in business before the last syllable was out of the woman's mouth. He'd hit the redial button before he reached the door.

"Church on the Circle—God bless. This is Kim."

"Grace Harrison, please." He impatiently waited or her to come on the line.

"Hello, this is Grace. How may I help you?"

Her voice was warm and welcoming.

"Hello?" she said again.

Speak.

"Grace? Jud Marlowe here."

"Oh, hello. I got your message. I tried calling but your cell phone must have been shut off."

"That's okay," he replied. Sweetness and light, he thought. Well, it's not going to work with me.

Silence on both ends.

"Jud?"

"What?" It came out gruff.

"*You* called *me*," she reminded him softly.

"I wanted to set a time to interview you," he said, all business now.

"Okay. What's your deadline?" He wasn't the only one who was all business. He could hear her flipping pages.

"I need to interview you today or tomorrow at the latest." He paused and then added hesitantly, "I also wanted to tell you something." He had decided that the direct approach was his best chance. He needed to win her trust as soon as possible if he had any prayer of ferreting out her father's news before somebody else did.

The paper shuffling stopped. "What?" she asked.

"I don't see any way that I can keep you out of a story about the program." When the silence lengthened, he added, "I thought you should know that."

"And, if I refuse?"

"I'll write the story anyway."

She remained silent. He tried waiting her out, recognizing the power game she was playing.

Seconds passed.

"This is ridiculous," he said finally.

She actually laughed and that surprised him. "I know. The equivalent of a telephone version of seeing who will blink first, isn't it?"

Jud relaxed. "So, do we get together or do I go after this on my own?"

"Very well. I'll do the interview—about the program."

That was a little too easy, Jud thought. "What's the trade-off?"

"I'm doing a little research of my own, for the programming at the church. I'd like to ask you some questions as well."

"I thought I talked a lot last night. Too much for a journalist who was supposed to be interviewing you."

"I thought you left things out," she replied. "Besides, starting with the date was a little like starting with step three. How about I bring along the initial bio form we use so you can complete that—strictly as an exercise for the article, I mean?"

He hesitated. "Okay, but just be warned that this time, you'll do most of the talking, and face-to-face, I never blink first."

"Fair enough. How does three this afternoon suit you?"

"Great. I'm meeting Suni at noon, but after that—"

"Okay, I can give you an hour at three, of which I want thirty minutes to interview you."

"About?"

"Well I'm going to pre-screen you for the program and then we can discuss when you'll be ready to get together with Elaine."

"Elaine?"

"The woman you met last night?"

"Oh, *that* Elaine. You know it was just an interview—you set it up yourself. I called her last night and clarified a couple of things."

"Still, she indicated on the response card that she would like to see you again. She made a point of it even though she knew you weren't in the program."

"Why? I mean, I'm not…that is, well, I'm not exactly…"

"Her type?"

"That and I really don't fit the profile for the program, if you get my meaning."

"Ah. Well, actually that's part of my research. You have the background for it—childhood religious training, attendance at a church-sponsored college, and so on. Why exactly did you fall away?"

"Why did you end your engagement?" he shot back.

"My engagement has absolutely nothing to do with an article on the program," she replied coolly.

"Exactly. And, as nice as she is, I'm not interested in seeing Elaine or having you work your matchmaking wonders on me."

"Fine," she said and he thought he heard a hint of laughter in her tone. "So, what's your angle, for the article?"

Again suspicious of her giving up so easily, he took a minute to consider his next move. What was *her* angle, he wondered, and why was he spending so much time on this nothing story when he had far bigger fish to fry? He thought of half a dozen reasons why he should cut bait here. Surely there were any number of ideas for Valentine's stories in a city this size. Stories that he could write in his sleep and leave him free to pursue the more interesting hard news story about the two senators. But to get close to the senators, he needed Grace.

He cleared his throat. "I'm considering focusing the story on David and Suni," he said.

"Really?"

"You sound surprised."

"No, it makes sense, but can you be objective? I mean, David is your friend, right?"

It was the second time she had challenged his ability to remain objective. Was it a deliberate reference to the Blackwell fiasco? She had to have put it all together—his name and the story unfavorable to her father. Grace didn't strike him as the type who would hold a grudge, but he hadn't been the best judge of people's nature lately.

"On the other hand," she continued, warming now to the idea, "if you and Elaine get together, then you'll have both ends of the spectrum—the couple just beginning to get acquainted and the couple who have found their match. It might just work."

"Hmm, you think?" The words were out before he realized he'd uttered them aloud.

Grace ignored his sarcasm. "You did like her, Elaine?"

"She was okay. I'm just not in the market...."

"But I was thinking that for you to have the full effect of the program..."

"Wouldn't that be an injustice to Elaine? I mean, she's serious about this, while I definitely am not."

"The quintessential confirmed bachelor?"

"Something like that."

Grace hesitated. "Okay. Perhaps you have a point about Elaine," she said. "The last thing anyone in the program needs is to go into a relationship thinking about changing the other person."

"Elaine is doing that?"

"Maybe she was thinking about it."

"Then the match wouldn't work, right?"

He saw that she didn't want to let it go, but finally she said, "I guess not."

Jud felt the thrill of a small victory and decided he could take a more benevolent tone with her. "Look, here's an idea. Dave tells me that you accompany him and Suni when they go out. What if I tag along a couple of times? I can see how it works with people who know me and won't be intimidated by having a reporter observing their blossoming romance. Then I can add interviews with the others and we have a dynamite piece."

There was another long moment of silence while Grace considered this. He wished he could see her face. "Let's see how things go this afternoon," she said.

"Okay. Three at the church then?"

"Actually, how about the Y? I usually head over there for a workout around then?"

"You want me to interview you while we're running on a treadmill?"

"That's one option. Or we could find a spot in the lounge, which is pretty quiet in the late afternoon. We could talk and then I could work out after."

* * *

The lounge at the YMCA wasn't just quiet, it was deserted. Grace handed Jud a bottle of water and led the way to club chairs near the window overlooking the handball courts. She was in her workout clothes: shapeless sweat pants and a cropped—as in literally cut off with a pair of scissors—sweatshirt. It was her normal workout attire and yet she wished she had taken the time to put on something more attractive.

Of course, that would mean owning something more attractive, she could hear Bethany telling her.

She curled into the chair, took a long swallow from her own bottled water and then a deep breath. She had spent a good part of the afternoon preparing for this meeting, but now that it was here, now that he was only three feet away, his long legs stretched out in front of him, invading her space….

Oh, stop it! You're acting like a junior high school kid with her first crush.

I do not have a crush on Jud Marlowe. I've known the man less than two weeks.

No, but you are attracted—as any normal woman would be. Now, what was it you wanted to say to him?

Grace cleared her throat and sat up straighter, her legs folded beneath her. "Let's start with the bio and pre-screening interview and go from there."

"Are you determined to set the agenda here?"

"I just was suggesting a possibility."

"Okay. You quiz me first and then I get to interview you—uninterrupted."

Grace realized that her initial assessment of him had been right. He did indeed have the most terrific smile.

"It just seems to make sense to do these prelim questions first. It will help me to better..."

"Control the story?"

"Not at all. I was just going to say that it would help me better understand the approach you might want to take. At the same time it will give you a much better view of how the program works."

"Okay. Shoot."

She hadn't missed the millisecond of hesitation or the expression behind his smile that clearly said, I'm willing to play this game for now, but let's not forget who the reporter is here.

She smiled and grabbed a form from her duffel bag, which he immediately took from her.

"Better yet, let's kill two birds at the same time or however that old saying goes," he said. "I'll ask you the questions. That way, you can enhance the information by telling me more about what you might be looking for in the way questions are answered."

She started to protest, but he'd already pulled out a pen and inserted her name at the top of the form.

"No need to bother with address and such. Okay, how did you hear about the program, Ms. Harrison?" He waited. "Come on, Grace. After all, it's not Watergate, it's a simple little Valentine's Day story. Let's lighten things up and have some fun with it."

He had a point. The sooner he got what he needed for the Valentine piece, the sooner he'd be out of her life. She pretended to search her memory. "Well, let's see, I think I first noticed an announcement in the church newsletter."

"Where were you born?"

"In Washington."

"Ah, a native daughter. That's rare. Date?"

"June ninth, 1974."

Jud completed the next questions himself. "Gender—female. Height?" He studied her. "Five-two."

"Five-four," she protested.

"Weight? One hundred and ten."

"Eight," she corrected.

"Hair is brown—coffee with just a hint of cream," he said, filling in the information.

"Or mousy brown if you want to be really honest." She touched her hair self-consciously.

"Eyes? Blue—no debating that. Very blue." She watched as he wrote both words in the space provided.

Grace blushed. He hadn't even looked up from writing in her hair color. He had actually remembered that her eyes were blue. *Very blue.*

"Education…" She watched as he filled in her degrees and majors. "Occupation…" Matchmaker, he wrote in his strong confident script. "Marital status…" He glanced at her puzzled. "Marital status? Why would you ask that?"

"People do get divorced or widowed, Jud."

"Yeah, but…"

"But you didn't think our program would take such people? We're trying to be inclusive, not exclusive."

"Good point." He waited with pen poised. When she didn't respond, he repeated, "Marital status?"

She smiled. "Single."

"Do you have children?"

"Not this week," she replied and he laughed.

"Would you like to have children?" He paused. "Now, there's a great question."

"Yes. Would you?"

He frowned and then focused on the form. She put her hand on his, stopping the pen. "You're the one who said it was a great question, so answer it."

He swallowed hard. "Sure…maybe…I don't know. I haven't thought much about it."

"At your age, you should. Think about it, I mean," she added, feeling a flush of color tint her cheeks. "Next question?"

He was obviously as relieved as she was to get back to the form. "Okay, mark all that apply."

She took the form and pen from him and studied the list, calling out each item as she marked it. "I am not dating anyone seriously now. I believe in marriage. I am shy. I am active. I enjoy quiet evenings." She handed the form back to him. "And you?"

He scanned the list. "Too busy to meet people. New in town. Active. Outgoing."

"Dating anyone?"

"Dating," he said, making it clear that he would go no further, as he turned the page. "Okay, on to part two. Who is your ideal match? Starting with age range."

"Between twenty-five and forty."

That gave him definite pause. "You'd get involved with a younger man?"

She laughed. "Well, let's think about that. Would you not get involved with a younger woman?"

"Okay, double standard. Moving on. What about general attractiveness—physical qualities?"

"Inner qualities are more important."

"So you'd be okay with someone shorter or someone really heavy or bald or…"

"That depends. I try not to judge books or people by the packaging. And you?"

He grinned. "I'm afraid I'm not quite so virtuous. The package is important—inside and out."

"Oh." Grace couldn't think what else to say because she was dealing with the realization that she probably didn't measure up. Why on earth that should even enter her mind was beyond her.

Jud cleared his throat and returned to the form. "Last question: name the three most important factors you'd consider before dating a person."

"Integrity, intelligence and faith-based values. How about you?"

"Intelligence, sense of humor…" He paused as if struggling to come up with a third. "I'm afraid you got me once again. The first thing that comes to mind is looks. Not quite as noble as your faith-based values."

Grace settled back in her chair and pushed her glasses back up the bridge of her nose. "I know you said that your parents brought you up in the church, so forgive me if this offends you, but do you believe in God?"

"We've done that bit, remember?"

Dodging the question.

"Okay. Do you attend church?"

"Yes."

Too quick and way too succinct.

"Regularly?"

"Yes."

Okay, this is getting us nowhere. Grace smiled and leaned slightly forward. "Really? Which church?"

He hesitated.

"This is just idle curiosity, Jud, not part of the quiz," she said softly, but he didn't relax.

"I just moved here a short while ago. I'm shopping around, I guess." He was beginning to sound defensive.

"Sorry for the third degree. It's just, as I've mentioned before..."

"Several times," he said with a grin.

"Even if all you're doing is reporting a story, I believe that someone with at least a passing acquaintance with the tenets of a firm religious faith would better understand what we're trying to do."

"I once did an article on starving people in Africa and I didn't have to starve or go to Africa," he replied.

"Even so."

"Look, Grace, based on what you've told me so far, this program of yours can open doors for people. Important doors related to finding the perfect life partner or as close to it as anyone comes in this world, right?"

"Go on."

"From everything I've been able to put together in terms of background so far, it delivers—at least for some people—and for others it offers new friendships and opportunities for getting out there beyond the job."

"All true. What's the point?"

"I just don't think that the journalist telling this story adds anything by being a card-carrying true believer. In fact, just the opposite. A skeptic like me writing the story gives it more validity."

"Touché," Grace said. "By the way, in your church search, have you visited the Church on the Circle?"

"Not yet, but I hear they have a dynamite coffee-house and a really cutting-edge program of adult education."

She laughed and he relaxed. "Okay, your turn." She checked her watch. "Thirty minutes, Mr. Marlowe."

Chapter Six

Jud turned over the tape in the recorder, leaned forward and fired his first question. "Do you really think this matchmaking thing is good for people?"

"It does work, Jud," she assured him. "I've seen wonderful results. Oh, it's not always moonlight and roses or wedded bliss, but sometimes it is and for every couple who finds that level of happiness there are two or three more who find solid and lasting friendships. Either way, connections are made."

He grunted.

"I could get you some statistics on the success of the program, or just ask David."

"I'll take the stats and also ask Dave," he replied.

"You are such a cynic," she said, but now she was the one who was more at ease. "Okay, next question. What do you want to know in particular?"

"Let's start with David and Suni," he said.

"David joined the program several months ago."

Grace laughed at the memory of that first visit. "I don't think I've ever seen someone so nervous and, at the same time, so determined."

"I understand he had some mismatches before Suni."

"He told you about that? Every one, though it was a mutual parting of the ways. He's remained friends with two or three women. Two of them have since made matches of their own and David has been there to celebrate with them."

"What happened when he met Suni?"

"You must have covered that when you talked with Suni earlier?"

"Yes, but I want your take on it. I'll probably also ask the same question of David and perhaps Bethany."

Grace nodded and smiled. "Their meeting was so magical. I doubt there was a person in the room who couldn't see that they were meant for each other."

"On both sides?" Jud asked. "I mean I know that from David's point of view, this was a done deal from that first night. What about Suni?"

"It was the same for her. She's a bit more reserved about it all, but no less enthralled with having found her one true love."

"You believe that? I mean in general, the one true love bit?"

"Absolutely. I believe that for every person God has created the perfect life partner. The challenge is for those two people to find each other."

Jud grinned. "That would be God giving answers in the form of choices?"

"You're beginning to catch on," she said.

"Okay, getting back to David and Suni. Tell me where things went from that first evening at the coffee-house."

For the next half hour she gave him enough generic information about the progress of his friend's romance to write a small book instead of a simple article for Valentine's Day.

"I hate to cut this short," she said after glancing at her watch, "but we've gone longer than I scheduled. I still have to work out and I have a meeting tonight."

"As in a date?"

"A meeting," she replied firmly and stood up.

"I just have one more question for now." He stood as well. The recorder was still running. "I know I've asked before but have you ever considered using the program to find a match for yourself?"

"I don't meet the criteria," she said with a smile when he had expected a flash of temper.

"You're kidding. You don't practice what you preach— no pun intended—I mean on the faith-based bit?"

She could see that his reporter's brain was spinning with the possible inclusion of that little scoop in his ar-ticle. "Oh, make no mistake about it. My life is firmly rooted in my faith," she said.

"Then what criteria don't you meet?"

"I'm not in the market for a lasting relationship. So, it seems that we are two of a kind. Hey, maybe your idea of tagging along on some dates with Suni and David might just work. I'll call you with a time and place."

* * *

"Marlowe, wait up."

Jud had barely made it to his desk before he turned to see Millie beckoning to him from her office. He knew she was going to ask about the Valentine assignment, not because it was of headline importance, but because he was still on trial and she'd made it clear that she would be watching him closely.

"So, how's the piece coming?" she asked as soon as he reached her office. Millie led the way inside indicating that he should sit. Obviously she was expecting more than a simple update. He prepared himself for another of Millie's coaching sessions. "What's taking so long? The art department is waiting. Surely you've settled on an angle by now."

"A matchmaking service," he replied.

Millie made a face. "Old news. This is your best shot? What about that reception I sent you to at the Capitol?"

"I heard about it there. A friend of mine has used the service, and so has the daughter of a prominent diplomat. Her parents want her to find a husband who isn't after her for the family fortune."

Millie was still not convinced. "Has some potential, I guess. Of course, it could be some kind of scam, which would, of course, be a whole different story. How do you know the person in charge of this so-called dating service is legit?"

"She is," he assured his editor. "And it's a matchmaking program. There's a difference."

Millie blinked in surprise at his tone. Then she sighed—one of her patented "have-I-taught-you-nothing" sighs. "Not good enough, Marlowe. Who is she? What's her background? How did she get into this? More to the point, what does she get out of it? How much does it cost?"

He started with the last question. "It's a free service."

Millie stood and began pacing the office. "Free? Nothing is free."

"It's a church program."

"Touchy ground, Marlowe," she warned. "Sex, politics and religion—even for us." She shook her head slowly. Everyone in the office knew that meant she was about to kill the story. "Why don't you move forward with the parks commission piece? I'll do you a favor and hand this off to Sara, perhaps for a woman's point of view."

He thought about the chance to take an assignment for Lifestyle and turn it into a front-page opportunity. "A couple of other people I know, including one here at the paper, have actually used the service—*successfully* used the service," he added.

He'd played his first ace.

She walked over to the glass partition that separated her office from the rest of the newsroom and studied her staff. "Somebody here?" Millie loved office gossip.

Jud nodded.

"No kidding," she muttered more to herself than to him as she returned to her desk. "Interesting. Any names among these contacts of yours?"

"Ambassador Ashraff's daughter."

Millie was disappointed. "I see. You know the more I think about it, Sara would be a better fit for this piece. She'll have to play catch-up but she's perfect. Why don't you bring her up to speed and get back to what you do best? Commission hearings, that sort of thing."

"Did I mention that the program is the brainchild of Senator Riley Harrison's daughter?"

There. Second ace played.

Please don't make me have to give up the potential for the Gordon angle.

Millie's eyes widened and she actually smiled. Millie almost never smiled. "Grace Harrison? Really?"

Jud nodded and held his breath.

Millie pinned him with her give-me-the-facts look. "I knew you were holding out on me, Marlowe."

Jud had the good sense to give her a sheepish grin.

"So, exactly how does this matchmaking thing work?"

For the moment, she had dropped the tidbit that Harrison's daughter was involved. But Jud wasn't kidding himself. He knew he'd have to face that later, but for now he hurried to give her the basics of the program. Millie listened intently and made a couple of notes as he talked.

"I tried the ten-minute date thing and I can see how—for some people—it might work. It certainly makes it easier to move on to someone else without the usual hurt feelings if there's no real attraction."

"How did you make the connection to Grace

Harrison?" Millie tapped her pen against the edge of her desk.

"I met her at that Capitol thing."

Millie's eyes widened and she stood and closed the door to her office. "You're telling me that Grace was there?"

Uh-oh. Too much information. Jud reluctantly nodded.

"Marlowe, Grace never—and I do mean never—attends any political function unless her father asks her specifically to be there."

Play it cool. "Really?"

"You met him? They were together?"

"No, I didn't meet the senator. As for being together, they're father and daughter, so in that sense..."

"Who was he talking to while you were talking to her *and* who made the first contact? You or Grace?"

"I...we just started talking and I'm not sure who all the senator talked to. He was working the room." Jud struggled to hold on to what he'd seen until he'd had a chance to build his story, but Millie wasn't the managing editor of a growing paper for nothing.

She came around and perched on the edge of the desk so that she was practically knee-to-knee with him. "Did Grace Harrison approach you?"

"She was also working the room." It sounded lame even to him.

Millie gave a hoot of a laugh. "The woman can smell a reporter at fifty yards. She knew exactly what she was doing in approaching you. The question is why."

Jud fought to keep his expression neutral, to give away nothing. He obviously failed, but at least Millie made the wrong assumption about his reaction. "If you thought anything else, then you're not just naive, you're downright arrogant, Marlowe. Grace didn't come up to you because of that dimpled smile of yours. She had your number and from where I'm sitting it looks like you let her play you."

Jud's temper flared, triggering his innate instinct to prove and defend himself. He took a moment to regain control. "I'd like to follow the story on her matchmaking program and see where it leads," he said quietly. "I can get close to the senator."

Millie studied him for a long moment then nodded. "Keep Grady in the loop. He's following the rumor about Gordon's party switch. Come up with something he can go with and you'll share the byline." She walked back around her desk, sat in a chair that had seen better days and stared at him as she tapped her pen against her desk.

Yeah, that'll happen, Jud thought. This is my story.

"How much time have I got?" he asked.

"As much as it takes to make sure that we break the story ahead of any other news service. You get Grady some concrete leads and we'll talk about a move to more interesting assignments."

"And if I don't?"

"Well, then I hope you like sitting through meetings of the Parks Commission because you'll be doing that for a long time."

Jud's heart hammered. This was it. He grinned at Millie, stood and offered her his hand, which she ignored as she pulled a file out of one of the tottering piles on her desk and started to flip through it.

"Marlowe," she barked, "get back to work."

The meeting was over.

Grace couldn't believe that she was actually thinking of calling him—again.

Well, it's for the story and the sooner I help him get the information he needs.

Then why, she thought, do I find him so…

Attractive?

Now I'm channeling Bethany.

Which is not necessarily a bad thing.

"He is very attractive," she mumbled as she searched for his number. "The problem is that he's clearly been told that too many times. He's certainly not above using his charm to get what he wants."

Well, if you know that, then why fall for it?

"I'm not falling for anything," she said as she found the piece of paper where she'd scribbled his number. "I'm just trying to stay one step ahead of him."

Right.

Jud's cell phone rang as he walked in with his laptop in one hand and a bag of Chinese take-out in the other. He kicked the door closed and fished the phone out of his pocket. "Yeah."

"Jud?"

Grace. Well, well, well. Instead of the irritation he had felt a split second before, he felt a sense of achievement. This was the second time she'd taken the initiative—third if he counted the Capitol event. That had to mean something. "Hi. What's up?"

"You sound rushed," she replied. "Did I get you in the middle of something important?"

"Nope. Just walked in."

"So, you haven't eaten yet?"

"Not yet."

She let out a breath. "Great. Look, David, Suni and I are having dinner tonight. So if you're game I thought we'd all meet at the Froggy Bottom on Wisconsin. How does that sound?"

"In Georgetown?"

"That's right. Is that okay or we could try someplace else? It's just that it's easy to talk there."

"It's fine," he assured her. "What time?"

"Seven. And Jud?"

"Still here," he replied.

"It's Dutch treat—I mean, this isn't like a real…"

"Date?"

She laughed. "Well, yeah."

"How about my treat? That's why they created expense accounts," he told her and hung up, thinking that she had a nice laugh.

Okay, Marlowe, you might want to get a grip here. Her laugh is not the issue—getting the story is.

The phone rang again. Caller ID indicated David.

"Hi, David," Jud said.

"Hi." David sounded as if he'd lost his best friend.

"What's happened?" Jud asked, balancing the phone between his shoulder and ear as he stashed the Chinese food in the refrigerator.

"I don't know. This whole thing with Suni and her Dad is beginning to get to me, which is probably exactly what her father wants."

"But something specific has happened, right?"

"Yeah. We'd started seeing each other without Grace being there, you know, sort of accidentally on purpose running into each other. Now Suni says we can only see each other within the confines of the program." Glum didn't begin to describe David's tone.

"Why?"

"The other night after we left the church separately, we met up again and went to a late movie. She told her mom that she and Grace were going to a movie, but a friend of her mother's saw us there and mentioned it to her mother."

"Really? I can't see Grace going along with anything like that."

"She didn't know. Anyway, Suni's mom told her that we had to agree to never again go outside the guidelines her father had set..."

"Meaning only seeing each other with Grace present?"

David sighed heavily. "Yeah. If we promised, then she wouldn't mention the movie to Suni's Dad. Now Suni's worried how her dad will react if we become front page news."

Jud had to have this article in order to maintain contact with Grace. "What if I agreed to let you and Suni see the draft of the story before I file it?" It was something no reporter ever agreed to do, but it could buy him time.

"You'd do that?"

"Well, don't go spreading it around, but yeah, if it will help put Suni at ease."

"It might." David sounded a little better but a long way from fine.

"Hey, look on the positive side. Sounds like her mom is in your corner, right?" Jud reminded him. "After a few more weeks, enough time will have passed so you could go to her dad and ask for her hand—not to mention the rest of her."

"I guess. It's just that I've barely had a chance to give her a good-night kiss. I guess I can stick it out because…"

"Because you're crazy in love with the woman and you have this one shot at getting her father's blessing."

There was silence at the other end of the line.

"Yeah, when you put it like that," Dave replied grudgingly. He sighed again.

"Look, you're seeing her tonight, right? Froggy Bottom at seven?"

"How did you know that?"

"Because I'm a reporter, remember? And you guys are part of my story," Jud said. "Oh, yeah, and because Grace just called and asked if I wanted to come along."

"We're doubling?" Even as depressed as David was, he was excited at this news. "That's so cool."

"It's not a date, Dave. I'm working, remember?"

"Yeah, but how great to be just two couples out for dinner like normal people instead of having a chaperone. Grace is terrific, but…"

"Whatever. Hey, I've got to hit the shower. See you in an hour, okay?"

"Jud, about tonight? See if you can get Grace alone for a minute and see how she thinks things are going with me and Suni, okay?"

"Sure. Maybe I'll pass her a note under the table during appetizers," Jud said and then added, "Patience, Dave. It'll all work out."

David groaned and hung up.

He's late, Grace thought as she, Suni and David made small talk and studied the menus.

"I called Jud just after you did, Grace," David said as if he'd read her mind. "I'm really glad you asked him to join us, but I'm probably the cause of his being late."

"Me, too. I mean I'm so glad he's coming tonight," Suni added quickly. "Jud's a really nice guy, very special. Once you get to know him, Grace…."

"He's also a reporter gathering information for an article on the program," Grace reminded both of them.

"Of course," Suni said softly and returned to studying the menu.

"Maybe something came up at the paper," David offered as the minutes stretched on and Grace glanced at her watch for the third time.

"Why don't we go ahead and order?" she suggested.

They had just placed their order for appetizers when she saw Jud enter. He said something to the hostess that made her laugh as she pointed him toward the corner booth where they were sitting. Grace was stunned to realize that she was assessing her own appearance as well as his as she watched Jud cross the room.

He was dressed in khaki pants and a thickly woven turtleneck sweater. He'd handed over his leather jacket to the hostess. His hair was still damp—whether from his shower or because it was sleeting outside, she couldn't guess. He moved with a confidence that had heads turning to see if he was anyone important.

"And he's a hunk to boot," Suni whispered, making Grace all too aware of how she had been staring at the man. She smoothed her hands over her gray wool slacks and picked a nonexistent piece of lint off her pale blue sweater before looking up at him.

"Sorry I'm so late," Jud said as he slid into the spot next to Grace. It was the only excuse he offered. No explanations, just a simple apology. It was David who stepped up to offer a possible explanation.

"I was just telling Grace how I called just as you were trying to get ready and…"

Suni placed her hand on David's. "Well, he's here now and that's all that matters. Ah, sushi," she said as if the waiter had just saved her from a desert isle.

"Suni has been singing the praises of the sushi here," Grace said, handing him a menu. "Do you like sushi, Jud?"

"I've heard that it's kind of an acquired taste."

Grace laughed and felt the release of the tension in her neck and shoulders. "You hate it," she said bluntly. "Me, too."

Jud grinned, and Grace could see that everything was going to be fine. They were normal people. Just four friends out for dinner.

The waiter took their order. The salads arrived as David was describing his latest adventure working for a member of Congress. Grace made a comment about a congresswoman that had them all laughing. Then she looked at Jud in horror.

"I shouldn't have... For a moment, I forgot that..." She felt like an idiot. She'd been in this town all of her life. She knew better than to share stories about her father's colleagues or anyone else for that matter.

Jud put his hand over hers. "Hey, it was a cute story and actually very flattering —the congresswoman, but hardly headline news. Forget it."

"Nevertheless, maybe we should talk about the program," Grace said, freeing her hand on the pretext of passing David more rolls. It was unsettling enough to be sitting so close to him without having to deal with actual physical contact. "Suni, why don't you tell Jud more about what the program has meant for you."

"Of course." Suni nodded and then turned her attention to Jud. Grace was grateful for her intervention. *What on earth is the matter with you?* she thought, focusing on her salad.

"When Gracie rang that little bell of hers," David added to Suni's story, "I thought no way that was ten minutes."

Grace relaxed. "You even challenged me, as I recall."

David laughed. "Yeah, sorry about that."

"Dave's always been one to get caught up in the moment," Jud said and launched into a story from their days as college roommates when David had almost missed an exam because he'd gotten so engrossed in studying for it.

"Oh, like you never get involved with a story," David countered. "Once this guy was doing a series on inner-city kids in Richmond who wanted to be part of a city basketball league but didn't have shoes or uniforms. When nobody stepped forward to outfit them, Jud here helped them put together all sorts of projects like a car wash and collecting recyclables for cash until they had the money they needed. Those kids went on to win the league championship, but another reporter had to cover the story because Jud was out trying to raise enough money to get the kids to the state tournament."

Grace was surprised to see that Jud had become inordinately interested in his food. "That's really wonderful, Jud," she said.

He shrugged. "Not a good idea for the reporter to get so involved that he becomes part of the story," he said. "Oh, good. Here comes the main course."

Chapter Seven

The following Monday afternoon Grace was having trouble concentrating on the report she was trying to prepare for the church's Board of Trustees. Her mind kept wandering back to the dinner with Jud.

Not *with* Jud Marlowe, she corrected herself as she gave up on the report in favor of tackling some of the mounds of documents to be filed. Dinner with Suni and David. She transferred a pile of folders onto the office's only spare chair.

Okay, but start with the fact that things were different because Jud was there.

Only because he was working on his article.

Although he did seem to enjoy himself, she thought and smiled at the memory.

The fact remains, I made the first move. I called and invited him. Why did I do that?

She hammered the stapler with the palm of one hand as she organized sets of papers for filing.

The fact is that he accepted because of the story, so I really need to get over myself and stop making more of this than it is. I have more important work to do than worry about that man's motivations.

She shoved several stapled papers into an already overstuffed file. "He's a loose cannon and yet it's like You want me to notice him, help him," she said aloud.

Someone cleared his throat and she turned so quickly that a pile of papers teetering on the edge of her desk went flying.

"Grace?" Jud stood at the door of her office.

"Hi." She sorted through a flood of feelings that ranged from embarrassment at her clumsiness to being too aware of the way he dominated the cramped space. She really had to get hold of herself.

He bent to help her pick up the papers, glancing around as he did. "Who were you talking to?"

"God." She took the papers he handed her. "Thanks."

"God?" He raised his eyebrow slightly. "Sorry. I didn't mean to interrupt your prayer."

"I wasn't praying, just talking."

"To God." He was very close to grinning and working overtime to keep it under control.

"You can smirk if you like," she said. "You do it, too, talk to Him. Everyone does."

"Uh, not really."

"You may not talk aloud, but you talk. Call it talking to yourself if you like, but at the other end it's God listening."

"If you say so."

She heaved an exasperated sigh as she loaded more papers into file cabinets. "All right, I'll prove it. Has there ever been a time when you were working on a story and you had some doubts or reservations about it? About the way it was coming together?"

"Possibly."

"And in that moment, did you or did you not have an internal conversation about what you should do?"

He leaned against the door jamb and frowned. "Let me get this straight, you're suggesting that I turned to God for divine intervention?"

"Absolutely not," she said. "God raises the questions. *You* decide the way to go."

"Sort of no-fault religion?"

"It's called free will. God gives us the power to choose and hopefully we make the right choice. It's not that hard to recognize the right choice, just sometimes hard to make the sacrifice that choosing the right way will mean."

When he seemed at a loss for words, she turned her attention back to retrieving the scattered papers. She'd come dangerously close to bringing up the Blackwell story. She wasn't sure why, but it was important to her that when they discussed that it would be at his initiation.

Get a grip, she thought as she realized that Jud was now standing by her desk with a stack of papers and an uncertain smile on his handsome face. Handsome face? Why not just smile on his face?

"But you didn't come here for a theological debate,

did you? There's a chair in this mess somewhere," she said with a nervous laugh as she moved another pile of papers and books she'd deposited on the only other chair in the room. "What can I do for you?"

"I just stopped by."

"Not exactly in the same neighborhood as the paper," she reminded him.

He shrugged. "I had an interview not far from here." He seemed inclined to pace but there was no place to do it.

"Well, sit, please."

"I thought maybe you could take a break and we could go for coffee and discuss what happens once you have the questionnaire completed. Personal interview, right? I thought we could run through that for the article."

That smile should be illegal, Grace thought, feeling the now familiar flutter in her stomach whenever he directed it at her.

There were a dozen ways she could be nice about declining the invitation, but she didn't choose any. "Sure. Let me just get my stuff together here." Now, there was a Freudian slip. The only stuff you need to get together, lady, is the way Jud Marlowe seems to have of making you act against your better judgment.

She put several bundles of paper into her backpack and closed it. "I was about to head out for the day anyway."

He took the heavy bag from her. "Homework?"

"Yeah. I need to catch up on projects I've had to push

aside plus there's a lot of paperwork associated with the matchmaking program."

You're babbling. This is a mistake. He confuses you.

He held her coat for her and waited until she had turned out the light and closed the office door before following her through the main office, saying goodbye to Kim and Bethany, and then he opened the exit door for her. He was the perfect gentleman.

"I had a meeting with my editor," Jud said after they'd ordered and settled into a corner booth with their coffees. "She asked a lot of questions."

"About your article?"

"And about you."

"I see," Grace said softly. She could guess what was coming. Once again, she felt her heart plunge into disappointment. What was it about this man that made her keep hoping that he might be different? "Did she ask you to take an angle other than the David and Suni focus?"

"Millie rarely asks outright. It's more like she assumes."

"And you think that she assumes you'll know she wants the focus on me?"

He raked his fingers through his short charcoal hair. "Surely you can understand that *you* are the story here. It's you our readers want to read about. Keeping you— who you are—completely out of it is impossible"

"We agreed that promoting the program was the focus. You said yourself that it's a story that deserves telling."

"I know."

"I also thought I made it perfectly clear that I would not cooperate with a story focused on me."

"You did, but—"

"Then nothing's changed. Tell your boss she assumed wrong. Tell her no."

It was the kind of response that was clearly nonnegotiable.

He bristled. "No?"

She set her coffee mug on the small table between them and leaned forward. "Tell Millie Peterson that I won't have you use the program as a way of getting a scoop about me. Better yet, I'll call her myself."

He stopped her. "No. Wait."

She realized that she was more upset than the occasion warranted. Being around him seemed to do that to her. Still, she couldn't seem to control herself when it came to challenging his motives.

"Was it a coincidence that she just happened to send you to that reception, Jud?"

His strong chin jutted forward stubbornly. "Absolutely. That was pure coincidence. You were the one who wasn't supposed to be there."

She was impressed with how quickly he had turned the tables on her. She wanted to believe him, but she had seen the way he was watching her father and she had seen his eyes light up with anticipation once he realized who she was. Knowing that there was more to this than he was admitting, she decided to calm down and take a different approach to convincing him to see things her way.

"What if I told you that Suni's father thinks the story is a good idea?"

"He knows about this?"

"Yes, I told him."

"Why?"

"Because I saw no reason not to. Trying to keep things from the people involved is not a smart move, I've found."

"And he's okay with it—my doing a story about Suni and David?"

"He believes that having their romance in the public eye will place a great deal of stress on the relationship."

Poor Dave. "I'm afraid I don't get that. Why not just say he doesn't approve of David?"

"Oh, he approves. But if their love can survive public scrutiny and speculation, then the ambassador believes it has a better chance of standing the test of time."

"And what if the opposite happens and their love is destroyed?"

"It won't happen."

"It might."

She smiled at him. "Then that becomes the story—*Matchmaker Fails to Match These Two Hearts*. Millie will love the twist."

After they had sat in silence for a moment, she decided to say what had been on her mind for days. "Look, if this is going to work at all, we need to get something out in the open."

"By 'this,' do you mean the story or this?" He waved his hand between the two of them.

There is no *this* in terms of us, Grace thought. Is there?

"The story," she replied firmly. "Millie's assumptions aside, let's talk about your take on the story."

He sat up straighter, on alert for any traps. "You're asking the questions here."

Grace swallowed hard and plunged in. "Well, it's just that I've always had the feeling that you were never really excited about doing the Valentine's Day piece. Then when you met me, you got this idea that you could make it into something else. Something about me—or more likely my father. Is that accurate?" She couldn't recall a time when she had wanted to hear an answer less.

To her surprise, he didn't try to deny any of it. Instead he nodded. "You have to know that I didn't have a clue that you'd be at the Capitol that day. I'd just been handed this assignment—another probation check by my boss to see if I could deliver without messing up." He took a deep breath. "I never meant to upset you. I'm sorry for that." Jud watched carefully for her reaction.

So I've been right all along. I understood that before, but after the way he was the other night at dinner…

Grace tried to conceal her disappointment. "I'm not upset. I'm disappointed, although I have no idea why. I should be used to this and I should have seen it coming."

"Why disappointed?"

"Because I allowed myself to believe you were different. I've let my guard down and I know better."

He seemed genuinely at a loss for a response to that.

"So, you had 'messed up' before?" Grace prompted.

He hesitated, obviously deciding just how much to reveal to convince her. He took a swallow of his coffee and said, "Big-time. The Blackwell land deal in Richmond?"

She let out a long breath. Finally he was going to tell her. It was as if she'd been waiting for this. "You were the journalist who broke that story."

"'Broke' being the operative word." He took a moment as if the memory still burned. "You knew, didn't you?"

She nodded. "What happened?"

"I trusted a source without checking the motives of the source. I didn't make the connection between her association with Blackwell and her desire to pursue a personal vendetta. I'd always been able to rely on her before. She backed up her version with documents, but only gave me the photocopies. The clock was ticking. The evidence looked legitimate—even to the paper's fact-checking staff. We were all convinced that we had the goods and would get the actual documents by the time the story ran. So, I filed the story and because my editor trusted me, he put it on the front page."

"You got fired."

"Yes."

Grace waited for him to continue. When he didn't, she asked, "Who was she?"

Jud glanced up. "Nobody," he replied tightly.

"Somebody you trusted, you said that yourself. Was there more than just a professional relationship?"

Jud shrugged and looked away.

Grace sighed. "You were in love with her."

"We dated. I thought that she…" He paused and swallowed hard. "It never occurred to me that she was capable of such betrayal."

"So, how did you end up working for Millie?"

He let out a deep breath. Relieved no doubt that she had decided to move on to another topic.

"You know what they say—it's not what you know, it's who you know. Hal, my former editor, and Millie are friends. In spite of my mistake, he liked my work, and thought I deserved a second chance. Millie gave me that."

They drank their coffee in silence. She compared his version of events to what she already knew.

"Did you know that Charlie Blackwell is a friend of my Dad's?"

"Yeah. The senator's name came up in my research. I'm surprised your Dad didn't warn you to keep your distance from me when you told him I was doing a story on the matchmaking thing."

"I just told him that Millie's paper was doing a feature. He respects Millie so he didn't ask who the reporter was," Grace said and then looked up at Jud. "But Millie knows that we met at the reception?"

Jud nodded. "It slipped out."

"And, knowing Millie, she was all over it the minute the words *Grace Harrison* left your mouth, which is why she's pushing you to put the spotlight on me instead of the program."

"So, you can see the problem."

Grace paused. "I see the problem for me and my father, but what's your problem? You've potentially stumbled on a story that could lead to bigger and better things for you."

"Without your cooperation?"

"You said yourself that you could get the story with or without my help. A major exposé would certainly redeem your career. Of course it all depends on how you decide to position the facts."

"You really have this thing about reporters, don't you? To you, we're all bad guys."

"Not all, but it's a business where temptations can be great."

"What if I told you that it seems I'm developing something of a conscience," Jud replied with a wry smile. "Maybe it's David being my best friend. Maybe it's you. Maybe it's maturity and growing soft. Whatever the cause, I felt I owed it to you to let you know the truth." He paused and when she didn't say anything added, "It's okay, Grace. You don't have to sugarcoat it. I know you can't help me with the piece now."

Grace unwound her feet from under her and stood. "I'm going to give you three pieces of advice, Jud. Number one, never use another person to salve your guilty conscience."

"I'm not," he protested.

"Yes, you are. You want me to let you off the hook by refusing to take your calls and give you any further help with this Valentine story. Forgive the pun, but you never really had your heart in it. You just thought it would lead to finding some dirt on my father."

"I—"

"Now you realize it won't. And when it's not your best work, you can blame it on an uncooperative subject."

"You're backing out?"

"Actually, the way I see it, your story is good for the program and for David and Suni so I have every reason to want you to finish the assignment. And since, on the surface at least, it's about the program, there's not a lot you can tell people about me that they don't already know. After all, it's a simple little Valentine's Day piece for the Lifestyle section, right? So, figure it out and stop playing games with me."

With my heart, she thought and swallowed hard against the knot in her throat.

She could see that he was smothering a smile, which she found absolutely infuriating. "And that brings us to number two. Stop trying to back-door your subjects and people who might want to see you succeed and you might find yourself doing a lot better work."

"Like who?" His smile vanished, and his own temper was now on edge.

"Oh, let's see." She ticked the names off on her fingers as she listed them. "Your old boss, Millie, David, me." She hadn't really meant to say that last name out loud.

The smile returned. "Why, Ms. Harrison, I didn't know you cared. And number three?"

"You and only you can decide what you really want out of all this."

"Why would you want me anywhere near you or your family now that you know what I did before?"

"I told you. I've known who you were from that day we met at the Capitol. I recognized your name—names of people who are unfair to my father tend to stick."

"So again, why would you cooperate on anything I'm working on?"

"Because I have faith that the Blackwell situation was a turning point for you, Jud. You have a choice now. I'm hoping you make the right one."

"Don't bet on it," he said.

Now it was her turn to smile. "I'm not a betting person, Jud. Whether you want to acknowledge it or not, you have God on your side."

"I sure didn't see God pulling any strings when I took the fall for the Blackwell fiasco."

"Ha! Where do you think Millie Peterson's connection to your old boss came from?"

"Maybe the newspaper world is a pretty small neighborhood, especially in this part of the country?"

"Believe what you want. You're only wasting time and making it harder on yourself to figure out your next steps." She took their mugs and got refills for both of them before curling back into the chair.

And just like that, everything was back to normal between them. Comfortable. Easy. The way it had been that night with Suni and David. That evening together had been such fun, especially when Jud had insisted they all go for ice-cream cones and eat them while strolling along the nearly deserted streets of Georgetown, peering in the windows of the shops and galleries. She recalled now that she'd thought it was really sweet of him to find a way to give Suni and David some time alone by walking with her ahead of them, even if they were only a few feet away.

After they had put Suni in the car her father always sent to take her home, Grace, David and Jud had walked on for several blocks. Jud had enlisted Grace's aid in assuring David that things were on track to work out with Suni. Again, it was as if they were old friends.

"I was thinking of having a small dinner party at my parents' house," Grace said, her thoughts returning to the present. "Just David and Suni, Suni's parents and mine. And you, of course, if you're available. It would give you the opportunity to meet Suni's mom and dad. I would think you'd need that as background for the story."

"You're sure you can trust me in your home?"

"Some things we just have to take on faith, Jud."

Outside, it started to rain, one of those bone-chilling D.C. winter rains, but they barely noticed. Waiting for the rain to let up became the only excuse they needed to move from coffee to dinner by ordering soup, sandwiches and two glasses of water as they kept right on talking. The conversation turned to parents, more specifically to Jud's.

"I'll put my mother up against yours any day of the week," Grace challenged when Jud mentioned how delighted his mom would be to think he was actually doing a story about a matchmaker.

"You're on. Within five minutes of meeting you, she'd want to know why the matchmaker hasn't found a match for herself. Notice the subtle way I once again worked that question into the conversation?"

Grace ignored his attempt to probe her social life. "From what you've told me, I think she'd be way too preoccupied with hiring me to find someone for you."

"Touché." He raised his water glass in a toast.

"You must have had girlfriends," she said as she polished off her turkey sandwich. "I mean, besides—"

"Charlotte. It's over. She did me a favor."

"Okay. So have there been others?" Is there someone now?

"Sure, but I learned my lesson. Nothing serious. I date—a lot—but I'm just not ready to settle down, you know?"

"You just haven't met the right woman. Believe me, your mother is right about one thing. When you meet her, you're going to tumble right off that bachelor pedestal."

"Is this part two of the questionnaire process? The part where you interview me face-to-face?"

"Well, you wanted to give it a try, right?"

He hesitated and then grinned. "Why not?"

"Okay. Let's see. Usually we start with 'What community activities do you participate in?'" she said.

"I'm new in town, remember? Between the job and finding a place I could afford to live, I haven't had a lot of time for community activities."

"Hmmm. We'll move on." She took a sip of her water. "On a scale of one to ten with one being not at all and ten being absolutely, how would you rate yourself in terms of being emotionally prepared for marriage?"

He nearly choked on his water when he heard the question. She pounded him on the back and waited.

"Well?" she prompted.

"I don't know. Emotionally prepared? What does that even mean? If I met the right woman, maybe a five or six. I mean, if the question is whether or not I have the emotional maturity to handle being married...?" He waited for an explanation.

She sat silently, waiting for him to continue.

"Five," he said finally.

"Explain that. Tell me more about your idea of marriage, and the idea of you being married."

"You don't really ask these exact questions, do you?"

"We do."

"No wonder you have a shortage of men in the program," he muttered and bought time by cautiously taking another drink of water. "Marriage is something I believe in. One day I hope to find the right woman and start a life together, but there are things I need to take care of first."

"Such as?"

"Such as getting my career back on track so I have something to offer, some security for us as a couple."

She nodded. "What else?"

"It's scary—marriage, the responsibility of it, the unknowns."

"Now that's a really interesting choice of words." She leaned forward. "What unknowns?"

"Well, think about it. You meet somebody and date them over a period of months or even years, but during all of that you're both kind of on your best behavior. There's still that possibility that the other person will change, that this isn't the person you thought you knew."

Maybe he's not as over Charlotte as he'd like to pretend, Grace thought.

"That's why the principle of the program is so important," she said. "At least when two people in the program meet, they are assured of certain common ground when it comes to beliefs and convictions."

"I guess," he said, sounding anything but convinced.

"Okay, here's an easier question. Which of the following words would you use to describe yourself? Ambitious?"

He nodded.

"Demanding?"

"Nope."

"Organized?"

He grinned. "Judging by the looks of your office, more organized than you are."

"Romantic?"

"Absolutely."

"Stubborn?"

"So I've been told."

"Attractive?"

He actually blushed.

"You be the judge," he said, then cleared his throat and concentrated on his food.

"What are your goals?"

"Personal or professional?"

Grace smiled. "How about both?"

"Professionally, I'd like to get back to doing hard news, investigative reporting, stories that make a difference."

"And personally?"

He seemed at a loss for words. Finally he shrugged. "The usual, I guess. Settle down eventually—with the emphasis on 'eventually.' Family, the American Dream."

"I think Charlotte hurt you far more deeply than you're willing to admit," Grace suggested.

"Perhaps. On one level," he agreed.

"What level?" For reasons she couldn't explain it was important to her that he talk about Charlotte and his feelings about what had happened.

He laughed but the sound held no genuine humor. "You're not going to let this go, are you? Okay, then on the level that I had prided myself on being a good judge of people. Charlotte put that in doubt and along with it my confidence in my ability to separate fact from fiction in my personal life as well as my work."

Grace started to say something, but he went on. "Am I over her and what we had as a couple? Definitely."

"And doubting yourself, getting back that confidence?"

"That'll take a while."

They sat in silence for a moment. Finally Grace cleared her throat. "Moving on then. How regularly do you attend religious services?" He had answered this question before, but she thought he might be more honest now.

He glanced up, a huge grin on his face. "You don't give up, do you? I would have to say that I attend on an irregular basis."

"Because?"

"Work, time, other things get in the way."

Grace paused. It had never occurred to her that anything could get in the way of her time in church. She looked forward to it, planned for it, found it a much-needed part of her day. "Really?"

"That and needing some time to work things through after I lost my job."

"But why wouldn't you turn to God to help work things through?"

He lifted an eyebrow as if it were perfectly obvious.

"You can't possibly blame God for what happened?"

He looked out the window. "Let's just say that God wasn't available."

"He's always available," she said.

Jud made no attempt to reply.

She felt momentarily at a loss. These days she really didn't come in contact with too many people who were not solidly devoted to their faith as a key piece of their daily lives. She tried a new tactic.

"Isn't your faith—the faith your parents raised you in—a respite for you in times of stress?"

"I don't think much about it that way. Going to church is…"

"Not just the formal act of attending services. What about feeling God's presence in your daily life? Turning to Him when you're upset or happy or thankful?" Grace had believed herself to be completely tolerant of the fact that formal church membership and attendance might not be for everyone, but God as the center of daily living—how could anyone not feel that presence?

Why did she feel so strongly about this, about Jud feeling the same way toward God as she did?

Jud seemed dumbfounded by her questions. "Look, when you've seen how people treat each other—and I'm not just talking about what Charlotte did to me— I'm talking about the way the world really is. Neighbors turning against neighbors, friends against friends, allies against allies—and for what? Stupid stuff like a pair of shoes or the right to paint a fence purple or over a barrel of oil."

"But there must be times when there's nothing there but the foundation of your faith?"

"Well, sure, there are times like on 9/11 or when my sister's kid was in the hospital last year or…" He paused for a moment as if he realized he was beginning to sound defensive and was determined to regain control. Finally he said. "Guess I fail as a candidate for your program."

Grace reminded herself that this was purely an exercise. Jud wasn't really applying to be a candidate for the program. Lighten up.

She pushed her plate aside. "Anyway, those are the questions we would ask you. Then we would ask about the match you are seeking."

He leaned back in his chair and relaxed a little. "Such as?"

"Occupation, education, interests, that sort of thing."

He considered this for a moment and then ticked off answers on his fingers. "Occupation—not a biggie although I'd hope it was something she was passionate about, like I am about the news. Education—to me that does matter if you're going to be able to converse on an equal playing field, so either college degree or remarkably well-read. Interests? The key there is that she's open to new things. Of course, hopefully she likes sports and can ride a bike and not get bummed out by a ten-mile hike."

Grace measured herself against each answer and felt enormously relieved that she met every criteria he named.

"Well, it's good that you know what you want," she said, using her business voice to offset the flush of pleasure she felt at the idea that she could fit that bill.

"But I failed the interview, right?"

"Not necessarily. Sometimes the people we interview are not aware that they want the same things others in the program are seeking. Sometimes, the faith element has been pushed so far to the back burner of their lives that it disappears. But it's still there, simmering."

His gray eyes narrowed. "And you think that's the case for me?"

"I do." She had never been more sure of anything.

He shook his head, looking at her as if she might just be the most naïve person he'd ever met.

"I'll prove it," she offered.

"This, I have got to hear," he replied, folding his arms across his chest.

"You may have fallen away from regular attendance at services, but you said yourself that you turn to God."

"Grace, there wasn't a person in America who didn't turn to God on that horrible September day."

"Agreed. But you also turned to God—not the doctors—when your sister's child was in the hospital." She smiled triumphantly.

He laughed and shook his head in disbelief. "You are seriously reaching, lady."

"I mean it. I'm sure that I can find the right woman for you if you want to give it a serious try. Maybe it's someone in the program."

"It's not someone in the program," he replied. "Trust me on that one."

"But you hit it off so well that night with Elaine."

"Drop it, okay? Don't get me wrong. She was a winner—funny, terrific looking, smart, but not for me."

"You just met her. Give it time."

"Not interested and you're contradicting yourself. A minute ago you made it sound like the earth would move the minute I saw Ms. Right."

"Well, yeah, in a perfect world...."

The conversation stalled as if neither of them could come up with anything else to say.

"Rain's letting up," he said, glancing out the window.

"Oh, look at the time. I should get going." She started to gather her things, reaching for her wallet as he picked up the check.

Jud waved aside her offer to split the bill. "Once I file the story, you can take me for coffee," he said as he picked up her backpack. "So tell me—I mean stop me if I've asked this before—how is your search for Mr. Right going?" He laid money on the table and waited for her to lead the way to the door.

"Give it up, Marlowe. My prince will come along in God's good time."

"Well, you and God wouldn't want to rush into anything."

She realized he was teasing her and gave him a punch in the arm.

"Ow," he protested. "You've been spending way too much time at that gym, lady."

Outside the café they stood in the doorway watching the fine mist fall. Grace turned up the collar of her coat.

"Wait here. I'll get you a cab," he said.

"Oh, let's make a run for the metro," she said as she linked her arm in his. They dodged pedestrians and puddles as they raced to the nearest subway stop.

Laughing and completely out of breath, they caught the train just as the doors slammed shut. The car was jammed with rush-hour commuters and they found themselves pressed close to each other as they swayed in time to the rhythm of the moving train.

Conversation was impossible. Jud pushed a damp curl away from the corner of her eye and tucked it back behind her ear. She smiled up at him, then stopped smiling as their eyes met and Grace saw mirrored in his the same bewildered gaze she knew Jud was seeing in hers.

Chapter Eight

"So?" Bethany said as soon as Grace answered the phone.

"Hello to you, too," Grace replied, shaking out her jacket from the rain.

"Okay. Hello, Grace. Did you have a good day? Is your mom back from visiting your grandparents? How's your Dad? Oh, and how did it go with Mr. Tall, Dark and Oh, So Handsome?"

Grace laughed. "I had the usual good day, thank you. Mom got back last night and Dad, as always, was delighted to have her home. Let's see, what was your other question?"

Bethany let out a strangled cry of frustration. "You are driving me nuts, girl. You know very well why I called, why I've been calling for the last two hours. I tried your cell, the office and your house. Nothing. Where were you anyway?"

"We had coffee. Then it started to rain and so we decided to get a sandwich and wait it out."

Bethany sighed. "That is *so* romantic."

"And you are *so* easily impressed," Grace replied. "I often think that you should do the matchmaking for the program and I should just handle the paperwork."

"If I can match you with him, I'm more than happy to quit while I'm ahead. Have you seen the way he looks at you? Have you seen the way you look at him?"

"He looks at me the same way he looks at any subject for an article. Don't mistake salivating over a story that includes Senator Harrison's reclusive daughter with anything close to interest on a romantic level, Bethany."

"That shows what you know. The man is definitely interested in you. He's just not sure why. It's really hard for a guy to understand why he's attracted when you seem determined to mask any sign that you're a beautiful woman. The poor guy's confused."

Grace paused in the action of emptying the dishwasher. "There is nothing wrong with the way I dress," she said firmly. "Just because I buy good quality traditional pieces that last beyond one season…"

There was another pause before Bethany said, "Can we all say together, 'Bor-r-ring!' Frankly, and I say this with only your best interests at heart, you have no fashion sense."

"Between you and Mom always on me, it's like the two of you think I dress like a street person," she said, appalled at how upset she was getting over this old debate.

"Hey, it's not like that. A little color is all we're saying. Could it be that you're getting so upset because something has come into your life to make you think there may be something to this—or should I say *someone* has come into your life?"

Now it was Grace's turn to issue an exasperated sigh. "I give up. Thankfully Jud needs to file his article by the end of next week so we can all get back to our normal lives."

"Oh, you naive child," Bethany said, clucking her tongue as if she were Grace's disapproving teacher. "So, you had dinner. What'd you talk about?"

"We had sandwiches," Grace corrected. "We talked about the article."

"The entire time? What's he working on? A six-part series?"

"We talked about other things, normal small talk. His family." Grace laughed. "His mother sounds terrific. He says she's completely given up the subtle approach. She's determined that it's time he married and settled down. And his sisters are no better."

"Really? Finally, this is getting interesting. So, Jud is on the hunt."

"That's crude and no. His mom thinks he should be, but he's not interested." She stressed each of the last three words to make a point.

"There's something you're keeping from me," Bethany said.

"Okay. There was a woman and it was serious but she betrayed him."

"Sounds gothic. How exactly did this betrayal come off?"

"She was his source for the story on Charlie."

Bethany was unusually quiet, but the moment passed. "I see. So, you ate sandwiches and then?"

"We walked to the Metro and took the Red Line to Metro Center where I transferred to the Blue Line. End of report."

"Not so fast. You walked to the metro? In the rain?" Bethany sighed again.

"Actually, we made a mad dash. The only heavy breathing you need imagine was our being winded from running and almost missing the train."

That's not exactly true, she reminded herself. There was that look.

"Are you listening to me?" Bethany demanded and Grace realized she had missed her friend's last question.

"I just don't understand why you're so intent on Jud," Grace said. "After all, you don't really know him and usually you're the one warning me not to trust the media."

"I've just got a feeling, okay?"

"Whatever," Grace replied. "How are things with Nick?"

They talked for another twenty minutes with the focus on Bethany and Nick, caught up on what had happened at the church after Grace left for the day, and then made plans to get together for the weekend.

"Well, see you in church," Grace said, then added, "unless, of course, you'd like to meet me at the gym at seven?"

"See you in church," Bethany said firmly, then added, "unless you'd like to meet me at the mall at ten?"

"Give it up, Taft," Grace replied, but she was laughing as she hung up.

"This is it," David said as he and Jud worked out on the treadmills two days later. "I'm going to ask Suni's father if I can marry his daughter ."

"Aren't you rushing things?" It wasn't that Jud hadn't expected this, but he'd thought it would take longer. David married? He and Jud had been the last holdouts in their group of friends. Now he would be the lone single guy and the pressure on him was about to double.

"The ambassador has been officially recalled. It's now or never."

"What does Grace say?"

"She agrees, even though she'd like us to have a little more time."

"How are you going to do it? Do you even know Suni's parents?"

"Grace introduced us when Suni and I first started seeing each other, and, of course, I see them every Sunday."

"Every Sunday?"

"Church and then Sunday lunch at their house."

"So that's why you can never make the game on time," Jud muttered. "I thought that business about going into the office after church was weak. I just couldn't figure out why you felt the need to make excuses." He couldn't believe how depressing he was finding this news. His best friend, college roommate, fantasy football partner, the man he could always count on to be right there for Sunday afternoon touch football games and Monday night NFL broadcasts. All of that was about to end. He couldn't remember when he'd been more depressed.

"Isn't it terrific?" David said. "I don't know when I've been more nervous and excited at the same time."

"Yeah, Dave, it's great."

Stop feeling sorry for yourself, Marlowe.

David was oblivious to Jud's bad mood. "Thanks. Guess this means we'll have to start working on a match for you. Hey, how about Grace? You two seemed to hit it off at dinner the other night."

"Dave, forget it," Jud snapped, then grinned to soften the reprimand. "Hey, I'm still out here having a good time playing the field, remember? Trust me, I can handle things, but thanks for the thought."

"You're not having fun. You barely go out other than for work, and you stopped being able to handle anything when Charlotte dumped you and trashed your career as she left."

"Drop it, okay?"

But Dave was on a roll. "A wife is different from a date, Jud," David said solemnly. "A wife is a forever kind of thing."

Tell me about it, Jud thought. A life sentence. He resisted the urge to shudder. "Right. Let's just concentrate on you and Suni for now."

David beamed with anticipation of the prospect. Jud didn't have the heart to ask what he would do if Suni's father turned him down. "And speaking of that, I've got a story to file," he said instead, turning off the treadmill and slapping David with a towel as he headed for the locker room.

Of course, the good news was that if Suni's father gave his permission for the marriage, Jud had a terrific ending for his piece. His mood had brightened considerably by the time he reached the newsroom.

But his good mood was short-lived.

"Marlowe," Millie called as soon as she spotted him. "My office."

He was barely inside the door before Millie started. "Have you been checking the web? There should be more chatter out there. What have you found out about Harrison?"

"Nothing new and certainly nothing concrete."

Millie looked defeated. "You haven't been able to uncover anything while hanging out with Grace?"

Jud squirmed slightly. "It's not as simple as it seems. You told me yourself how savvy she is. She's already suspicious about me using her as a conduit to the senator. This is going to take some time."

"Time's not a luxury we enjoy in this business. The drums may be quiet at the moment, but you know as well as I do that there's somebody working this angle at every media outlet in the beltway. And you can count on it that somebody is getting close. That somebody had better be you—and Grady."

"I'm on it," Jud replied.

Millie obviously had her doubts. "Really? How come Grady was surprised when I asked him how this was going? He says you haven't given him zip or even discussed what you know about the Harrisons with him. Do not make the mistake of trying to back-door me, Marlowe."

It was the same thing Grace had warned him about. Trying to go behind the backs of his supporters to get the story. He had to give Millie something. "I'm having dinner at the Harrison home next week."

Millie's thick brows shot up. "Well, well, well. I am impressed. Gracie must really like you." At the mention of Grace, her features actually softened slightly. "She's a good person. I hate that you're going to break her heart."

"Who said anything about that."

"Oh, stop with the aw-shucks routine. If you shave twice a day and put on an actual suit, you're anchorman material and you know it. You've got half the interns around here drooling every time you walk by."

"Grace Harrison is not some intern," he said hotly.

Millie smiled. "Ah, so it goes a little both ways or are you just feeling protective, sort of a big brother thing?" Then she shrugged. "Look, I like her, too. She and her father are two of the good guys, but they also understand the game. Just try not to let her fall in love with you, okay?"

Once again he was dismissed as Millie picked up her phone and punched in a number. On his way back to his desk, he was aware of a couple of the interns smiling at him as he passed. Okay, so he was all right in the looks department, but Grace Harrison? Surely she was smart enough to appreciate that she just wasn't his type. After all, the woman was a professional matchmaker and he wasn't ready for commitment. Plus there was the two thousand pound gorilla in the room—the faith-based issue.

Grace glanced at the table. There were no glasses. How could she have forgotten the glasses? Earlier, she had forgotten to buy lemon for the fish she was preparing and had to run back to the store. She had given Mary the housekeeper the night off because she wanted to do it herself. Now she had set the table with no glasses. Was everything else in place? She took a quick inventory. Napkins? No napkins. Good grief.

She paused and took a deep breath. "Okay, what's going on here?"

I'm just nervous. Just need to relax.

"I have given dinner parties for ambassadors, world leaders. I've even cooked dinner for a president—of course, it was before he was elected, but I did it. These are friends. It should be easier."

She returned to her survey of the table.

"Okay, so Jud's coming. But, it's because he's doing the story."

I really want this to work out—the story, I mean.

Grace checked on the appetizers and folded napkins for the table. She concentrated on polishing the water glasses and setting them precisely at each place.

"Okay," she said, giving the table one last look. "I have to get dressed."

I should call Bethany.

I can dress myself.

Maybe not. I'd better call.

Bethany was there within thirty minutes.

"You must have broken every speed limit," Grace said, still not sure why she'd called her friend.

"I hit the lights. Here, I brought along a couple of things." She deposited a large garment bag, stuffed to almost bursting, on Grace's bed.

"A few things? This is a department store."

Bethany shrugged and started unzipping the bag, separating the clothes into piles. "Now then," she said, standing back and surveying her work, "let's get moving. Strip."

"Excuse me."

"Come on." She checked her watch. "We've got an hour, maybe less. Your mom got home just as I arrived. She's handling dinner."

"I'm handling dinner," Grace protested.

Bethany gave her a look that said she was wasting time. "Yes, you decided the menu, prepared each dish, but this is your parents' home. I tried to get you to move into an apartment with me but you insisted on staying here with them. Your mom is perfectly capable of putting things in the oven and making sure everything is done. Get out of those clothes and put one of these outfits on."

Grace threw up her hands in exasperation and began considering the clothes Bethany had laid out on the bed. "Which one?"

"Blue, I think," Bethany said, more to herself than to Grace, and pulled a blue sweater and black leather pants from the pile.

Grace held up the leather pants with two fingers, then dropped them back on the bed. "Try again."

"You're right. It's too grand a leap." She rummaged through the clothes. "This one," she said, holding up a moss green silk dress with long sleeves and a slightly flared skirt.

"I can't," Grace protested, fingering the fabric.

"Sure you can. It's perfect for you and I can't imagine why I thought it would work for me. Try it on."

It was indeed perfect. The fabric skimmed over her shoulders and hips and settled with a soft floating sensation around her calves.

"Shoes," Bethany announced, holding up a pair of high-heeled strappy sandals in suede that were the exact color of the dress. "Ah, I do love that we are the same size from head to toe. Earrings."

"I can barely walk in these shoes and you want me to serve dinner? And these sleeves are bound to end up in the salad dressing and..."

"Earrings," Bethany repeated, holding up a pair of small gold hoops. "Now sit." As soon as Grace sat at the dressing table Bethany turned the chair so Grace couldn't see herself in the mirror.

"What are you doing?" Grace asked after Bethany

had spent several minutes styling her hair. "I don't have that much hair."

"Be still. I'm almost done." She sprayed a light film of hairspray and then gently applied liner to Grace's lids. "Okay, I guess you can do the lipstick yourself."

Grace turned to look at herself, reaching for her glasses. Bethany stopped her. "Not tonight, Gracie. Contacts." She opened a drawer in the dressing table and handed Grace the container as she stuck the glasses in her pocket and started packing up the rest of the clothes.

"It's too much," Grace whispered, but she couldn't seem to stop looking at herself. She looked good. No, she looked great.

Bethany grinned. "You look really terrific."

The doorbell chimed.

"Showtime," Bethany said softly.

"Call Nick and stay for dinner," Grace said, and it was more of a plea than an invitation.

"Looking like this? I don't think so." Bethany indicated her jeans and T-shirt and less than perfect hair. "Besides Nick's away on business. You'll be fine. Jud Marlowe, on the other hand, is not going to know what hit him."

The Harrison house had the kind of solid, rooted-in-tradition style that was a good match for the senator's political philosophy. The Harrisons had sent a car to meet him. The driver was a talker.

"You know the senator?" he asked conversationally.

"His daughter," Jud replied, unsure of why he would share that information with a total stranger.

The driver grinned at Jud in his rearview mirror. "'Bout time one of you young hotshots realized what a prize that lady is."

"I'm not. . . ." Jud had actually been about to deny that he was romantically involved with Grace—again to a total stranger. "I'm not sure what you mean." If the guy was inclined to gossip then maybe he would have some nuggets worth hearing. He checked the name on the license. Elijah Jones.

"I mean," Elijah replied, emphasizing each word, "that the lady is a real blue-chipper. You cannot find a more decent, caring, lovely woman than that, so if I was you I'd just stop looking."

Jud started to respond, but Elijah held up a warning finger, again making eye contact through his mirror. "But I'll tell you this right now, mister. Unless your intentions are serious, you might as well let me take you right back home."

Jud decided a change of conversational direction would be best. "You seem to know Grace very well."

The driver shook his head in wonder. "Grace saved me, my friend. Took me off the streets, got me cleaned up, taught me how to go for a job interview, helped me find this job. And at the time, she was no more than fifteen or sixteen. She was always doing stuff like that—getting others to do it, too. Made her folks crazy worrying about her, but made 'em mighty proud at the same time. That little lady is special."

Got it, Jud thought as they drove along tree-lined boulevards past increasingly larger homes with lawns like putting greens. "They say the apple doesn't fall far from the tree," he ventured, hoping to encourage Elijah to keep talking.

"You got that right. The senator and his missus are first class all the way. Not like some, pretending to care about the people when what they really care about is—"

"You know the senator pretty well then?" Jud had to do something to interrupt what he could see was going to be a long harangue.

"I've had supper with him and the missus—and Grace, of course. And I usually drive him to the airport. He asks for me special," Elijah replied, and the pride in his tone said that this was an honor equal to a Purple Heart.

"He must trust you."

The driver nodded. "He does at that. Time to time, he'll ask that I meet a party coming to see him when they need to talk privately, without making headlines, you know."

Like Senator Gordon? "Really? So you've had some big names riding with you?"

Elijah paused, glanced at Jud in the mirror and then turned a corner. "You could say that," he replied coldly as he pulled up to one of the more modest homes on the block and parked. "But I ain't about to name names, if that's your game, mister."

"I'm sure that's why the senator chooses you when

he needs special attention," Jud replied, offering him a generous tip. "Thanks for the ride."

Elijah refused the tip and Jud was halfway up the front walk when Elijah called to him. "Mister?"

Jud turned.

"I meant what I said about Gracie."

"Got it," Jud replied, unsure if he'd just been threatened or simply reminded of the origin of the conversation. Either way he could be sure that the next time Elijah Jones drove any member of the Harrison family, Jud was likely going to be a topic of conversation.

Riley Harrison answered the door. Jud didn't know why he had expected hired help, but he had, and that momentarily put him at a loss for words.

"Jud Marlowe?" Harrison asked. His tone was friendly but guarded.

"Yes, sir," Jud replied, offering the senator his hand.

"Come in, come in." Senator Harrison swung the door wide in a gesture of pure welcome and hospitality. He was a large, portly man with an impressive shock of red hair. His complexion was florid and he had features that made him appear perennially pleasant and approachable—one of the reasons behind his enormous popularity with voters well beyond his state.

Jud juggled the flowers his mother had insisted he bring. He was unsure of whether he should present them to the senator or continue to clutch them until either Grace or her mother made an appearance.

"Those for Grace?" The senator seemed to read his predicament and was having trouble smothering a smile.

"Yes, sir."

"Gracie," the senator called in the general direction of the curved stairway. "Company's arriving. Ah, Catherine, this is the reporter."

Grace's mother was slender with a cloud of dark hair and an expression of serenity that was the perfect complement to her husband's more expansive demeanor. Jud offered her his outstretched hand, which she took in both of hers.

"So glad you could come, Mr. Marlowe. Grace tells us that you and David are good friends. I'm sure having you here will help put him at ease. He's always a bit nervous around the ambassador." Then she turned her attention to the open door, where the senator was already halfway to the street as a sleek black sedan from the diplomatic pool pulled to a stop. "Please excuse me for a moment. Suni and her parents have just arrived."

Jud moved a little farther into the foyer and nearly collided with Bethany, who came flying down the stairs.

"I'll pick up the rest of that stuff tomorrow, Gracie. Oh, here's Jud," she called over her shoulder. "Hi, Jud. Bye, Jud."

Outside she kissed Mrs. Harrison, laughed at something the senator called to her and waved in the general direction of the black car as she headed for the driveway and her own vehicle.

Jud heard a noise and glanced up the stairway. Then he blinked and looked again.

Chapter Nine

Grace? He stood there staring up at her as she took a deep breath and attempted to run lightly down the stairs, looking as if she'd just stepped out of a store window. In the instant it took her to mimic Bethany's entrance, Jud noted every detail. Her dress was perfect—subtle but sensational in the way it fit and flowed as she moved. Her hair shone in the soft light of the chandelier, her face…her face was radiant. And he realized she wasn't wearing her ever-present glasses. She was—in a word inadequate to describe the transformation—beautiful.

"Jud, I'm so sorry. I—" The thin strap on one sandal broke and she slid toward him, tripping over her feet, her eyes wide with fear.

He caught her in something between an embrace and a bear hug and held on, the bouquet of pink roses and freesia crushed between them.

"Well, there's grace, the attribute, and then Grace,

the klutz," she said with a sardonic smile. "I told Bethany to forget the shoes."

Ah, so Bethany had had a hand in the transformation. He studied her up close, noting that the makeup was perfect in its subtlety. The lips were especially…

"Uh, Jud, I'm fine, really." She pushed herself away and sat on the bottom step to remove the broken sandal. Free of it, she turned to greet Suni and her parents, who had crossed the threshold just in time to see Jud holding Grace.

"Small mishap," Grace explained, lightly kissing Suni and her parents on both cheeks. "Fortunately, as someone once told me, clumsiness isn't terminal. Please excuse me while I change shoes and put these in water," she said, holding up the broken sandal in one hand and the crushed bouquet in the other. "There are appetizers in the living room."

She limped down the hall with an elegance that belied her one shoe on and one shoe off predicament, leaving her parents to resume their duties as hosts. The driver might have a point when it came to Grace Harrison, Jud thought. The lady was pure class.

David was the last to arrive—a fact that clearly did not endear him to Suni's father. He entered the room just as Grace's mother was passing around a tray of appetizers and the senator was refreshing everyone's beverage.

His apologies were rambling and profuse until Suni moved quietly to his side and placed her small hand in his much larger one. The effect was nothing short of astonishing. David stopped babbling and accepted Mrs. Harrison's offer of Russian tea.

"I believe that you and I have something to discuss, Mr. Forrester," Suni's father said formally, then turned to the senator. "Perhaps we might use your library for a moment?"

"My pleasure," Harrison boomed and indicated the room across the foyer.

"We could wait until after dinner, sir," David replied, glancing nervously at Suni.

"This won't take long nor delay the evening any further," her father replied and led the way to the library.

David had no choice but to follow, and as he passed, he cast a glance at Jud that reminded him of a man on his way to the gallows.

Suni took a seat close to her mother, who patted her daughter's hand tenderly. The senator and Mrs. Harrison looked at Jud with bright smiles.

"So, Mr. Marlowe..." Catherine Harrison began.

"Please make that Jud, ma'am." Great. You interrupted, dork.

Catherine smiled. "Lovely. Jud, do tell us how your article is coming along."

Her eyes and smile were as warm and unwavering as her daughter's. It was as if he was the only person in the room and she was intensely interested in anything he might have to tell her. Jud understood that she was asking him to help her relieve the tension that permeated the room.

"Yes, yes," the senator boomed, taking his wife's

cue. "I understand you work for Millie Peterson. Can't imagine what she thinks of a story on matchmaking. Millie usually goes in for something that she refers to as a little more edgy for that paper she's running."

"It's for the Lifestyle section," Jud said. "Even alternative papers occasionally need something a little more mainstream. It attracts new readers."

"Readers who might have decided the paper was too avant-garde for their taste?" The senator was smiling, but the guarded look was back. Grace had that look as well.

"Yes, sir, you could say that. It's like courting the voters. You have to offer a little of the conventional so that they'll at least consider the less mainstream."

The senator's eyebrows shot up and the slight nod of his head indicated respect. The guarded look didn't waver.

"The kid's quick," he said to Grace as she entered the room wearing flat black shoes and looking a great deal more at ease.

"He's not a kid, Dad."

The senator laughed. "Sure he is. You all are. Innocents at the very least. Why, in our day we had—"

The door to the library opened and Suni's father emerged, followed closely by David, who wore an expression as if he'd just been blindsided and wasn't sure if he remembered how to put one foot in front of the other. Grace, Suni and Jud instinctively moved toward him.

But Suni's father positioned himself at David's side,

one hand on David's back as he motioned for Suni to come forward.

"David Forrester has requested the hand of our beloved daughter in marriage." He paused as everyone held their breaths.

"And?" His wife finally blurted the first word she had said above a whisper all evening.

"I have agreed that this would be good." The ambassador placed Suni's hand in David's and crossed the room to retrieve his tea.

The room exploded in a chorus of congratulations, laughter, tears and a round of embraces. Jud ended up hugging Grace after he'd given David a celebratory high five while Suni and Grace hugged and did a little dance of joy.

"Isn't this a wonderful ending for your article?" Grace said, looking up at him and seemingly unaware that they were in each other's arms for the second time in less than an hour and in full view of her parents.

"Couldn't be better," he agreed, looking down into her eyes and realizing that a man could get lost in them. It was like diving into calm blue waters.

"Please say you'll be my best man?" David asked, clapping him heartily on the back again.

Jud reluctantly released Grace. "I'd be honored."

"Shall we adjourn to the dining room?" Catherine said and led the way.

The dinner conversation was far livelier than Jud might have expected when he first saw Suni's parents. It was as if now that the decision had been made, they embraced David as their son and any hint of stilted formality had disappeared. It was well-known that the senator didn't permit alcohol in the Harrison house, but that didn't stop the toasts from coming. Toasts with water goblets raised followed by toasts with coffee and tea cups after Grace, Suni and their mothers had removed the plates and brought in enough dessert to feed half of Congress.

"And are we not to be honored with a toast from the best man?" Suni's father asked once they had all feasted on chocolate pecan tarts, lemon squares and bite-size pieces of cherry strudel.

"Yes, a toast, Jud," Senator Harrison echoed, tapping his water glass with his fork.

Jud stood, raised his glass first to David and Suni and then turned to Grace. "To the matchmaker," he said quietly.

"Hear, hear," Senator Harrison boomed as they all toasted Grace.

Grace blushed furiously, dabbed the corners of her mouth with her napkin and said, "Isn't that the phone?"

They all became aware of the ringing and Grace excused herself to answer. The ambience shifted slightly, as if everyone waited for Grace's return while they kept up the pretense of continuing the festivities. Jud wondered if this was how it was for politicians and diplomats—every ring of the phone held the promise of news that could change lives.

"It's for you, Dad."

Jud saw the look that passed between daughter and

father and knew that Grace was telling her father that he ought to take the call. "It's Ken," she said.

"My chief of staff," he explained unnecessarily. "I won't be a minute," he promised and went into the library, closing the door behind him.

"Shall we take our coffee into the living room?" Catherine asked and the transition was effortlessly achieved as if there had been no interruption. By the time they had all moved to the living room, the senator was back, taking charge of the conversation as he teased Suni about needing the National Cathedral in order to host all the guests that would want an invitation to her wedding.

Jud couldn't help wondering what could have been so important that Grace wouldn't have simply taken a message. His journalistic curiosity was on high alert. He knew of no pending legislation or other senate business that might have brought a call that the senator would take in the middle of a dinner party.

As if on cue, Jud's pager vibrated. He checked it quickly. *Millie.* He'd better take it. "Sorry," he said. "Do you mind if I use your phone?" he asked Grace's mother. "It's my editor," he said, pointing to his pager.

"Of course. Use the phone in the library. I hope it's nothing urgent."

Jud smiled. "Probably a coup at the Parks Commission," he said and when she gave him the same blank stare her daughter had at the Capitol that first day, added, "I'm joking."

He didn't close the door. That seemed rude. Instead

he rounded the antique English desk that dominated the center of the room and called the number on his pager.

"How's it going?" Millie said when she answered on the first ring.

Jud bristled as he tried to control his temper. "Are you checking up on me?" he asked, trying to keep his tone light.

"Relax, Marlowe. I just wanted you to know that one of our sources reports that Senator Gordon has virtually gone into hiding. This could be it. Any sign that Harrison is in contact?"

Jud thought about the call the senator had just taken. He glanced at the papers on the large desk. He placed his hand on the stack closest to the phone. Stop it. He withdrew his hand as if the papers were a hot stove.

"Marlowe?"

"It's a dinner party," he said as he picked up a pencil and began to lightly tap it against the papers. He caught a word—a word and some numbers. The temptation to read what was in plain sight was incredible. He stood and turned his back on the papers, leaning against the desk and concentrating on getting rid of Millie as quickly as possible. "Look, my best friend just got engaged and it's going to make a great ending for the piece."

"Just keep your eyes and ears open, okay?"

"Got it."

Millie grunted—her version of signing off—and the line went dead. Jud turned to replace the phone in its cradle and knocked the pile of papers to the floor. Aware of the open door and the nearness of the others, he hurried to gather the papers and replace them as precisely as possible on the desk.

He looked up to find Grace and the senator standing in the doorway watching him.

"Everything all right?" Senator Harrison asked.

Jud was glad for the dim lighting in the room. He knew his face was flushed and that, to the senator, he must look as guilty as a basketball player who had committed a flagrant foul. "Yes, sir. Sorry about this." He tapped the last of the papers against the desk and added them to the pile. He knew that his voice sounded forced. He wished Grace would stop looking at him as if she couldn't quite make up her mind whether or not to believe him.

He was well aware of how close he'd come to crossing a line of decency—again. If she knew how shaken he was, she might look at him with sympathy instead of the suspicion and doubt he'd seen when she saw him holding private documents from her father's desk.

"I'm afraid I have to go." He moved away from the desk and resisted the urge to keep his hands in the air. "That was my editor, Millie. A new assignment." He had no idea where he was going, but there was no way he could make it through the rest of the evening. His heart was beating so hard he figured that Grace and the senator could hear it from across the room.

"Well," Grace said quietly, "you got what you came for."

Jud's stomach lurched. Did she honestly believe that

he would stoop to rummaging through her father's private papers? "Look, I'm sorry...."

She took a step past her father and toward him. She smiled. "David and Suni's engagement will be a wonderful ending for your article. I'll walk you to the door."

He felt breath rush back into his lungs. "Just let me say good-night to everyone," he said with a smile.

The senator stepped aside to let him pass and offered to call a cab for him, but Jud declined.

The senator studied him closely for a long moment, then led the way back to the living room where the others could be heard laughing. "Cathcrine, Jud has to leave," Riley called out. "I'm going to have to speak to Millie Peterson about giving the kid a break long enough to enjoy his best friend's engagement party."

"Dad, he is not a kid," Grace repeated softly, but she was smiling.

As soon as Jud left the house he realized what he had to do. He almost ran the two blocks to the nearby shopping area. He entered the local pharmacy. The clerk pointed him toward a pay phone in the back. Jud flipped through the directory until he found the listing he wanted.

He pulled out his cell phone and tapped in the numbers.

A woman answered. "Good evening."

"Hello, this is Jud Marlowe. I'm sorry to disturb you, but is Reverend Gibbs at home?"

"Yes. Just a moment."

In his interview with Timothy Gibbs, Jud and the

minister had made a connection—as men with common interests, as men with similar curiosity about the major issues of the day, and as men who had both stepped off the path in pursuit of success. Jud had been surprised to learn that before becoming ordained, Reverend Gibbs had worked on Wall Street during the heyday of the Internet stocks. The minister had confided that his own personal greed had led him to do some things he regretted. He'd left Wall Street, enrolled in seminary and never regretted it.

"Hello? Jud?"

"Hi, Reverend."

"How can I help?" The minister's tone told Jud that he understood that Jud was in trouble.

"It's not about the story," Jud rushed to assure him as if that would put the man's mind at ease.

"Where are you?"

"I just left the Harrison house."

"I see. Suppose we meet at the church in half an hour?"

"Yes, sir. That would be fine. I'm really sorry to have interrupted your evening."

"Half an hour, Jud. I'll leave the side entrance open for you."

"Thank you, sir." As he walked toward the Metro station, Jud gulped in the cool night air.

Maybe this is just a panic attack, he thought. He had suffered several following the Blackwell fiasco. But why? I didn't do anything wrong.

But you thought about it. You were tempted.

As he waited for the next train he began having second thoughts about the call to the minister. What am I going to say to the man? He's come out in the night to meet with me and all I've got is, what?

An old woman waiting for the train glanced his way and moved farther down the platform, clutching her bag.

Oh great, now you're frightening little old ladies. You are some piece of work, Marlowe.

With the date moved up for the ambassador and his wife to leave, plans for the wedding had to be put on the fast track. Bethany took on the role of wedding coordinator. Suni's father no longer insisted that Suni and David be accompanied on their dates, but they tried to include Grace and Jud in their plans anyway. Bethany urged Grace to use these opportunities to build her relationship with Jud.

"There is no relationship," Grace protested. "He's filing the story today. It runs tomorrow. That's the end of it except for the wedding." But was it? The image of Jud handling the folder still haunted her. Had it been an innocent mishap or had he pretended to drop the folder to cover the fact that he had been looking at it?

Bethany sighed dramatically. "It's about trust," she said as if reading Grace's mind. Do I trust him? Grace thought as she gave her friend a puzzled look. "I mean trust the signs," Bethany explained. "You are just bound and determined to ignore all the signs, aren't you?"

"Such as?"

"Oh, let me see if I can come up with one or two… dozen. You go to the Capitol reception and out of hundreds of people, who do you end up talking to for the greater part of the afternoon? And who just happens to be best friends with David? And who just happens to have been assigned a Valentine's Day story? And…"

"You're reaching," Grace said as she entered data on her computer in preparation for that evening's new crop of souls seeking a match.

"And who," Bethany said firmly, "has had the hots for you ever since he met you? Oh, he may not have recognized it at once, but trust me, I can totally visualize the look on his face the other night when he looked up that staircase and saw you." Her sigh sounded like an old-fashioned swoon. "Move over, Romeo and Juliet."

"Now you're really reaching." Grace saved the spreadsheet and sent the data to the printer. Sometimes Bethany lived in a fantasy world. The hard truth was that maybe Jud had used Grace. She forced herself to concentrate on anything but Jud. "How are things coming with Suni? Did she decide on a gown?"

"Nice change of subject. She wants you to go shopping with her—why, I cannot imagine. I offered to come and she accepted, but clearly thought that the two of you could manage."

"Well, I'm her maid of honor. Maybe she thought I would be hurt if she didn't ask me."

Bethany nodded absently as she added three more items to a list. "Can you do it this Saturday? Say, around three?"

"Sure."

Bethany beamed. "Great. Then afterward we can all go for dinner and discuss the plans."

"All?"

"You, me, Suni, David and Jud."

"Why on earth would you ask Jud to endure an evening of planning?"

"He's the best man."

"Uh-huh. Don't best men usually just take care of holding on to the ring and making sure the groom shows up?"

Bethany bristled slightly. "In an ordinary wedding, perhaps, but this is different. David and Suni want their dearest friends—that would be you for Suni and Jud for David—to share in the planning. Not to mention that we have less than six weeks to pull this thing together."

"Why do I get the feeling there's some sort of plot in all of this?"

"Moi?" Bethany feigned innocence. "Okay, so we're set for shopping and dinner on Saturday. I'll call the others."

After Bethany left, Grace studied the charts she had made for each of the new participants in the program. Six women and three men. She sighed. Hopefully after Jud's article ran those numbers would rise, especially for the men. She should call him.

She picked up the phone and dialed. "Jud Marlowe, please," she replied when the receptionist asked how to direct the call. Has it occurred to you, Grace Harrison, that you keep finding excuses to contact this man?

I just want to thank him for the article.

Right.

There was no use avoiding the issue. Either she believed he had given in to temptation or not.

A weak man—a dishonorable man would have looked through the files. Jud Marlowe was certainly not weak and she really wanted to believe that he was an honorable man.

Chapter Ten

"Marlowe." He sounded distracted and rushed, but Grace plunged ahead.

"I just want you to know that in the unlikely case that your article scares off any of the three men currently set to start the program this week, I will expect you to show up, register and become a full participant."

"And 'good morning' to you," he replied and his voice reflected his pleasure and surprise at hearing from her.

She couldn't find the words to ask outright about the folder. Instead she said, "You sound busy. Big story?"

"I wish. Just finishing up several projects—parks commission, a piece on the wonders of vitamin D and this matchmaking thing that's due in an hour. That one's the biggest problem. See, there's this woman who runs the program and she seems to have this idea that she can call the shots when it comes to what's in the story."

His banter seemed forced. "I see. But I'm sure that

you're prepared to show her who the boss is on this article." She was trying too hard to keep things light.

"Yes, ma'am. The media cannot have the subject of any article influencing its outcome. Talk about the tail wagging the dog."

"I understand. Still, my statement stands. Should this article in any way scare off perfectly good male candidates for the program, I'll have to insist that you step in."

"Uh, let me get this straight. You have strict faith-based criteria except when you're desperate for male victims...excuse me, candidates?"

She laughed. "Not at all. You have repeatedly told me that you have a strong foundation in faith. It may have been on the shelf a little too long, but that's not a problem."

His tone became more serious. "If you're really worried, call Dave. I showed him the article last night."

It seemed as good a time as any to bring up the night at her house. "How's it going with the assignment that Millie called you about the other night?"

There was a definite pause.

"That's...uh...the lead didn't pan out," he said. "Look, Grace, I wanted to apologize and explain. I know how it must have looked—me holding that folder. I accidentally knocked it off the desk and then just when I was putting it back the senator walked in. I can only imagine how it must have looked."

"Not a problem. Mom appreciated your call to thank her for the evening."

Catherine Harrison had done more than simply mention his call in passing. She had clearly joined Bethany's chapter of the Jud Marlowe fan club. "He's a lovely young man," she had told Grace.

"Mom, he's a reporter," Grace had reminded her.

"Well, it's not as if they are all piranhas. He's very handsome, don't you think?"

"Maybe, but that's not the point. He's a reporter getting a story, and a friend who wanted to help David."

"Still…"

Jud cleared his throat on the other end of the line. "Speaking of mothers, I don't suppose you'd be free this weekend? I know it's short notice, but if you're not doing anything…"

It was Grace's turn to pause—in abject shock. Was the man actually about to ask her for a date?

"I…uh…I think Bethany has plans for *both of us*," she said.

"Sorry. Bethany will just have to survive without me. It's my mom's birthday—a biggie. My sisters are planning a weekend of festivities and they're kind of pushing me to bring a date. You'd be doing me a huge favor if you agreed to come."

"Wow, when you put it that way…."

"I didn't mean that the way it sounded. I'd really like to see you, I mean without all the trappings of the article and David and Suni et cetera. It's just that inflicting my family on you first time out seems like a lot, but it would really be…"

"I'd love to," Grace said softly and for one single

moment thought she had only thought the words. Have I completely lost it? Just because the man might actually have found a way to keep you out of the article for the most part doesn't mean a thing. It just means the stakes will be higher next time. You owe him now. And you're going to meet the family and get even more involved?

Jud cleared his throat. "That's great. I'm warning you that my mom and my sisters will make more of us being together than you may want. They can come on pretty strong."

"I can probably hold them off for a couple of days," she assured him.

"Thanks, Grace. I really appreciate this."

"No problem. I'll let Bethany know that we both have other plans."

"And I'll call my sisters and get the details," he said. "Well, time to get this matchmaker piece filed. I'll call you later. Hope you like the article."

Matchmaker, Matchmaker!
Washington Singles Flock to Unique Program

When it's the most important decision of your life, you might need a little help. Fortunately, help is here in the form of a matchmaking program for serious-minded singles seeking the opportunity to meet their soul mates.

In the political and competitive hotbed that is life in the nation's capital, people will do whatever it takes to get what they want. Success is the name of the game and most young D.C.-ites relentlessly pursue it day and night. But when it comes time to find success in a personal relationship, who has the time or the connections to cut through the red tape of romance?

Enter the Matchmaker Program offered by the Church on the Circle.

This program takes things a step further. It requires participants not only to have reached the stage where they are ready for a permanent commitment, but also requires that all participants attest to serious commitment to a faith-based relationship.

"We understand what today's busy and exceptional young singles must endure in order to find a compatible life partner," states Grace Harrison, Director of Adult Programming and founder of the church's matchmaking program. "In our program, individuals have the opportunity to meet and get to know a number of like-minded individuals in a short period of time. This creates a solid foundation for finding the best possible match."

And participants agree. The program takes into consideration social and economic backgrounds, personality traits and individual preferences, as well as family values and interests. But by far, the bedrock of the program is the commitment to a religious faith.

"Matchmaking is an ancient practice that uses a process dedicated to providing the best results for all parties," Senator Riley Harrison's daughter reports. "We don't use computer matches or other impersonal tactics for making introductions between participants. Everything is face-to-face."

Further, this process allows participants to control what happens next. After every ten-minute introductory "date," each person is asked to sign a card indicating level of interest—from none to absolutely—in seeing the other party again.

"The fact that you don't waste a lot of time is a huge advantage," states one woman who asked to remain anonymous.

And it simply began as one woman's idea to make a difference for singles who are ready to move to that next stage. The program has now become an almost overnight success at building strong relationships through suitable introductions.

Let's not forget that faith-based criteria. "It's no different than people going to a bookstore hoping to meet someone," Ms. Harrison suggests. "You'd do that because you'd hope to find someone with a shared interest in literature or learning. What's so different about setting boundaries that assure you won't be wasting your time if you want to marry within your faith and build a marriage rooted in those basic values?"

But not every relationship works out, of course. "I've met several interesting men," reports Elaine

Bennett, a member of the program for several weeks. "And, while nothing has clicked in terms of everlasting, I'm delighted to have added some wonderful new friends to my social circle. Washington can be pretty lonely when your world narrows down to twelve-hour-plus workdays and trying to have a life on the weekends."

Clients come from a variety of backgrounds and cultures as evidenced by the unlikely match between David Forrester and Suni Ashraff. Forrester is a former college football star who now is chief of staff for Congresswoman Ruth Thompson. Suni Ashraff is the daughter of Ambassador and Mrs. Demendi Ashraff of Sri Lanka.

You'd think they'd be worlds apart, yet these two professionals met just six months ago when both signed on for the Matchmaker Program. Once they had been introduced, sparks flew—in spite of obstacles that might have been insurmountable. The ambassador and his wife had certain ground rules for their daughter in her search for an acceptable match. So the family had turned to Ms. Harrison—a family friend and former classmate of Ms. Ashraff.

Happily, everything has worked out for this couple. This reporter was privileged to be present the evening that Mr. Forrester sought the ambassador's permission to propose to Ms. Ashraff—permission that was granted. Because the ambassador and his wife have been recalled

to their homeland to accept a post in the government, the wedding is planned for six weeks from
today. Full disclosure: this reporter will serve as
best man.

"Happily ever after? Not always," reports
Bethany Taft, Associate Director of Programming. "But if you're looking for a safe and non-
intrusive way to find that 'match made in heaven,'
you should come out and see us."

If you're alone and lonely this Valentine's Day,
if you've tried the usual 'meet' markets with no
success, and if you're ready for a serious relationship, the program at the Church on the Circle
could be just what the doctor—not to mention
your mother—ordered.

Millie finished reading the article and gave Jud a
genuine smile. "Add the info on how to contact the
program and file it," she said.

Jud was stunned. He'd been preparing his case for
the moment when she scowled and said she hated it.

"Well?" she barked, looking at him over the rims
of her reading glasses and tapping her oversize wrist-
watch. She headed back to her office, then paused.
"Oh, and plan on covering the wedding, Marlowe.
It'll make a great follow-up. I assume I don't need to
remind you that it'll also be prime feeding ground for
picking up info on what Senator Harrison is up to?"

It took three of them—Grace, Bethany and Kim, the
church secretary—to field the flood of calls and e-mails

that poured into the church following publication of Jud's article. Within the first hour, Grace had all calls sent to the message machine and called Bethany and Kim to her office.

"We need a prescreening tool for the prescreening tool," she said, wide-eyed as she glanced down at the phone and saw all lines lit. "For now, why don't the two of you take the calls? Ask for name, phone number and e-mail address. Then gather the basic information we usually gather—just here through the sixth question. Tell them they'll be getting an e-mail or call back within ten days, okay?"

Bethany and Kim were grinning widely. "Aye, aye, captain," Kim replied with a sharp salute, as she rushed off to start fielding the calls.

"Bethany? About Saturday, I can't make it after all—and neither can Jud."

"Neither can Jud?" Bethany blinked. "It wouldn't be for the same reason, would it?"

"That's a bit of a stretch, don't you think?" Grace asked, tap-dancing for time.

"Maybe and maybe not." Bethany studied her closely. "Grace Harrison, you have never been able to tell even the tiniest of white lies in your life so out with it."

"We're going to his mom's birthday party."

As pleased as Bethany had been about the flood of calls coming in for the program, she was absolutely ecstatic at this news. "Wow! And you need to spend all day Saturday getting ready. I'll help—only this time you come to me. It's simpler than my packing up my entire wardrobe."

"Well, actually he's picking me up Saturday morning for the drive down to his parents' house. They have a small farm near Charlottesville."

"Cool. Friday, then. My place after work. We'll order in Chinese." She didn't wait for an answer but danced out of the room and up the stairs to the main office. Grace could hear her humming the "Wedding March" as she went.

"Gracie?" Senator Harrison was in the library when Grace got home from Bethany's on Friday. She was halfway up the stairs when she heard his quiet summons. Any time her father spoke in this kind of low subdued tone, Grace knew something had happened. She paused, torn between her desire to go to him and her equal need not to let anything spoil the way she was looking forward to the weekend with Jud.

"Hi, Dad," she said, retracing her steps and standing just inside the door of the library.

Her father smiled, but he looked tired and somehow older than usual. "Come in, Gracie. I need to ask you about something—about Jud Marlowe."

Grace tried to swallow around the sudden knot in her throat. He knew about the weekend. Her mind raced with explanations. *It's not as if I'm going away with him in the sense of spending the night with him. It's his* mother's birthday and I'll be staying in his parents' house and...

"Remember the dinner for Suni and David, when I got a call?"

Grace blinked and tried to comprehend what a call from her father's chief of staff could possibly have to do with her going away with Jud. She nodded and waited for more information—a trick her father had taught her and one that had served her well.

"As you may recall, Mr. Marlowe also used the phone."

"He was paged. His editor."

Her father waved his hand impatiently as if such details were unimportant. "So he said. In any case, he came in here to return that call." The senator spread his large hands over the desk, which now held nothing but an antique inkwell, a photo of Grace and her mother and a single manila folder.

Grace could see where this was headed—and the knot in her throat had now spread to her stomach.

"My call was from Ken and he gave me some important information. I jotted a few notes here on this folder."

"Sounds like Deep Throat," Grace said, hoping for a flicker of a smile from her father.

"The thing is that I left this file folder right here next to the phone, in plain sight." His eyes met hers and there could be no doubt of his conclusion.

"As you recall when we came to see about the noise we heard, Jud was handling this very folder."

"Of course, he had the folder. Jud had accidentally

knocked the papers and folders off the desk." Grace fought to remain calm, using Jud's logical explanation for her father's assumptions.

"So he said."

"Come on, Dad, you're imagining things." But she couldn't help recalling how startled Jud had been when he turned and saw both her and the senator watching him from the doorway. "Besides, if he had been looking for information and found it, wouldn't he have used it? Wouldn't he have rushed out of here and called Millie?"

He did rush out.

Her father frowned. "That's one of the things that has me so worried. He hasn't used it. What's his game?"

"He hasn't used it because he doesn't have anything," Grace replied. She picked up the folder and put it in front of her father. "How would he even have known the notes were important? It's an address and a date. No name or other notation. He would not been able to put together that this was something major."

Her father looked up at her. "Why are you so intent on defending him?"

"I'm not defending him. I'm simply looking at the evidence you've presented, which you have to admit is pretty flimsy." But her voice shook as she debated the issue with him.

Her father studied her for a long moment, then sighed heavily as he leaned back in his chair. "Ah, Gracie, you know better than to fall in love with a journalist."

"That's ridiculous," she protested and even to her

own ears her voice sounded slightly shrill. "I barely know the man. I'm just saying that you've hardly enough evidence to condemn him. Besides, you're the one who taught me everyone deserves a second chance."

"Grace, I liked Jud. I liked him in spite of the damage he did with that article about Charlie. We all make mistakes, especially when we're young and ambitious. After watching the two of you at dinner, it was also clear to your mother and me that there is something between the two of you. But the fact is that he's a reporter—a reporter trying hard to reestablish himself."

"You can't indict him on evidence that's so easily explained. He's just clumsy." She thought about their conversation. "While he was listening to Millie, he absentmindedly straightened some folders. He told me that she drives him nuts with her constant coaching and mentoring tips."

Her heart sank. She was defending him and even to her ears, Jud's excuse now sounded hollow. Her father was right. He'd been holding the folder. He'd been startled to see them. He'd left immediately afterward. He'd refused the offer of a cab. Why? Because he didn't want anyone reporting on where he'd gone or who he might have called?

Stop it. He explained himself.

"As of today, Senator Gordon has officially closed the door on any further discussion of a change in party loyalty," her father said quietly. There was no mistaking his disappointment.

"You can't believe that Jud had anything to do with that," Grace replied.

Her father shrugged. "Senator Gordon didn't give any reasons for backing away, but I do know that a reporter from *Washington Today* contacted him."

"Dad, I'm sorry."

The senator rose from his chair and came around the desk. He put his arms around Grace. "I'm the one who is sorry, Gracie. Sorry that I have spoiled this for you, but I do need for you to sever any further contact with this young man. Whether he took information or not, I don't think he can be trusted."

"I can't do that."

Her father's thick eyebrows rose in surprise. "Why not?"

Because I believe in him—in his integrity and desire to do the right thing in spite of his ambition. "I can't stop seeing him because we are both in the wedding."

"Ah, yes. Well, even so, he is not to come here again. Is that understood?"

"Yes." She hesitated. She was over thirty years old and still living at home. Until this moment that had seemed perfectly normal, but suddenly she felt like a teenager whose father didn't trust her. "I won't invite him here again until you are comfortable with that."

Her father nodded. "Thank you, Gracie."

"On the other hand," she said, stepping out of the hug, "he has invited me to be his guest for the celebration of his mother's sixtieth birthday and, even if I wanted to decline, it's too late."

She watched her father wrestle with the duality of good manners and his distrust of Jud. Then he smiled and pulled her back into his arms. "So it comes down to trust. For reasons I don't understand, you trust him. But you have to understand my suspicions—unsubstantiated as they may be—about Jud's lack of integrity on this matter."

Grace returned the hug. "Yes. Jud is a good man, Dad. I can't tell you how I know that, but I do. He may be struggling to find his way, but he wouldn't stoop to rifling through your private property."

"And I suppose that you plan to help him as he continues with that journey," the senator replied. He shook his head slowly. "Grace, you cannot single-handedly save the world. Believe me, I've tried."

Grace pulled away and looked up at her father. "I know. That's between Jud and God. I just won't give him up as a lost soul."

Chapter Eleven

In spite of trying to rationalize her father's suspicions, Grace found it impossible to pretend that his doubts hadn't rekindled her own. Could Jud have strayed yet again over an invisible line? She could barely concentrate on anything else the following morning on their drive down to the farm. They had exhausted the topic of David and Suni's wedding, as well as the incredible response to Jud's article, and were riding along in silence.

"How are your parents?" he asked. She was sure it was an innocent and polite inquiry, and yet all she could think of was that he might have used their hospitality to further his career. The more she thought about that, the more her father's suspicions seemed well-founded and the angrier she got.

"Mom is fine. She sends her regards. My father is disappointed."

Jud looked puzzled. "Mom sends regards but Dad is disappointed? In me?"

"You could say that. And, by the way, so am I."

He took his eyes off the road to look at her and the car swerved slightly. "You're upset with me?"

"I think I said 'disappointed.' There's a difference."

His defenses were on alert. She could tell by the set of his jaw, the slight twitch of a facial muscle, and the way his hands gripped the steering wheel. "This is the second time I've disappointed you. What have I done now?"

"My father…"

"I'm not interested in impressing your father," he snapped.

"Well, you certainly have no reason—any longer that is—to want to impress me." She stared out the side window at the passing scencry, fighting to control her own anger. She couldn't stop thinking about the fact that she might have allowed him to play her for the fool. After all, who had initiated most of their contact by constantly finding excuses to call him? Even when he'd ask her to come for his mother's birthday, it was a call she had made. Inviting her could have been an afterthought—or worse, a reward, because he'd gotten what he wanted.

Neither of them said anything for the next couple of miles. Then he let out an exasperated sigh and a laugh that sounded forced. "Okay, did I take a wrong turn back there somewhere and not know it? I thought we were having a good time and getting to know each other without the pretense of the article."

Grace had never been that good at containing her

feelings. "So you're saying that, in spite of all our conversations, in spite of leading me to believe..."

"Let's get one thing straight right now, Grace. I didn't lead you anywhere. You make your own choices, remember?"

"Are you seriously going to expect me to believe that every move you've made in these last weeks has not in some way been to find ways to get closer to my father through me?" She was shouting now. She folded her arms tightly across her chest and stared straight ahead, trying to calm down. She wouldn't give him the satisfaction of losing control. She forced a calmer tone.

"If you think I didn't see you stalking my father that day at the Capitol, then guess again, buddy. Why do you think I intercepted you and introduced myself?"

"I figured you were mesmerized by my irresistible charm," he said, but there was no humor, only suppressed anger in his tone.

"Ha. Another of your weak jokes. I was mesmerized all right. By my own ability to distract you. But you were never distracted, were you? Oh, no, you saw me and thought you'd found the mother lode—a perfect route to my father." She pressed herself more firmly against the door as if to put as much space as possible between them.

He kept his eyes on the traffic and said nothing.

"I notice you aren't exactly denying any of this," she said. "How anyone who had been betrayed as you were could turn around and pull the same thing is beyond my powers of understanding." She chewed on her lower lip in an effort to shut herself up.

Jud rubbed the back of his neck and kept glancing over at her as he slowed to a crawl behind a large truck as they exited the expressway. "Who are you, lady, and what have you done with Grace Harrison?" He was still trying to regain a semblance of the lighter mood.

Grace ignored the attempt as she struggled to hold in the tears that begged to give her relief from the suspicions that had been rekindled by the discussion with her father. Suspicions she'd suppressed after the conversation with Jud about the folder. The self-doubt and hurt she'd suppressed all night. Her father was right about one thing. Allowing herself to become involved with a journalist was stupid.

They passed a mileage sign indicating they were only a few miles from their destination. Why on earth did I start this now? Grace thought.

"Let's just forget it," she said.

He looked at her as if she'd suddenly grown a second head. "Just like that? Forget it?" Now he was the one who was shouting. "I don't know what you're accusing me of or what you think it is I've done, but let's get one thing clear. I asked you to come with me this weekend because I couldn't think of anyone I'd rather be with and because I couldn't think of anyone my mother would enjoy meeting more."

She opened her mouth, but he cut her off.

"*Not* because you are Grace Harrison, the elusive daughter of the famous senator, but because you are Grace Harrison, the first woman I have ever met who I was excited and proud to bring home to meet my family."

He turned off the main road onto a graveled drive that led through a grove of trees to a large old farmhouse framed in tall sheltering pines with fallow fields stretching beyond toward the horizon. It was the storybook picture of *home*. There was even a stream of smoke rising from the chimney.

"Don't you dare turn this back on me, Jud. All I'm saying is that for the moment we need to get through the weekend," she said.

"We're not done with this, Grace," Jud replied as he cut the engine and took a deep steadying breath.

"No, we're not, but I won't be responsible for spoiling your mother's celebration, Jud, so put a smile on your face and introduce me to your family." Grace opened the car door and waved to the throng of people and dogs who suddenly burst from the house and headed for the car.

Connie and Gus Marlowe were the very definition of down-home folks. Jud made offhand introductions as he busied himself getting their luggage out of the trunk.

"Mom, Dad, this is Grace Harrison. Grace, my parents, Connie and…"

"Gus," Jud's father said shaking her hand and grinning broadly. "Welcome, Grace."

Connie Marlowe put her arm around Grace and finished the introductions. "These are Jud's sisters—Eva and Jenny. Eva's married to Ted over there and those wild animals impersonating children are hers. Jenny and Brian are the parents of those two brooding teen princesses on the porch. I daresay we have achieved our goal of thoroughly embarrassing them by now."

Grace nodded, waved or shook hands as it seemed appropriate and didn't miss the nudge Eva gave her sister as the two of them grinned broadly at Jud.

"Any food in this place?" Jud asked, ignoring his siblings as he and Gus carried the luggage to the house.

"Didn't he feed you, Grace?" Gus called over his shoulder. "You'd think the boy was raised in a barn."

Connie hooked her arm in Grace's and led the way to the house while her daughters and their husbands corralled the younger children and the dogs. The minute they entered the front hallway, they were surrounded by a tantalizing medley of smells—herbs and spices simmering with the promise of a feast. The large harvest table in the dining room just off the foyer was set for twelve. The room opened into a kitchen that would be any cook's dream. Jud and Gus had disappeared up the narrow stairway.

"What can I do to help?" Grace asked.

"Oh honey, don't you want to sit by the fire and relax?" Connie asked, then grinned. "Well, of course, you don't. You've been cooped up in that car for the last couple of hours. Come on in the kitchen. I'm sure we can find something that needs to be chopped up."

From the moment they were out of the car, they were constantly involved with one or more members of Jud's family. There was no opportunity to get back to the argument, and Jud was frankly relieved.

The weekend flew by and as the time for the drive back to Washington grew near, Jud was surprised to realize that he felt regret that it was coming to an end. Grace had thoroughly charmed his family just by being herself. More than once he had heard her with his mother and sisters laughing and chattering like a houseful of sorority sisters.

The party on Saturday night could not have been a bigger success. His parents' friends had all gathered at the restaurant to surprise his mom, who thought she was going out to celebrate with just the family. There had been toasts and presents and stories that made Connie laugh and then cry.

Earlier that morning, on a trip into town, Grace had sent Jud and his sisters to fill the grocery list while she picked out a small gift for his mother at a local gallery. Just before they left for the party, she had given Connie a bookmark made from the ivory of an old piano key and hand-painted with a soaring bird. It was perfect. Jud's mother had studied to be a concert pianist. At lunch, soon after they arrived, she had confided to Grace that she was looking forward to getting back to playing for herself once she retired from her position as a high school music teacher.

Jud's youngest niece and nephew clearly thought Grace walked on water. After the party, when the children had been sent to bed with no hope that they would settle into sleep after the excitement of the evening, he found Grace up in the attic his dad had converted into a sort of dormitory for the grandchildren. She was sitting up in one of the beds, the younger children to either side of her and Jenny's teenaged daughters lying on their stomachs on neighboring beds, chins in their hands and eyes wide as Grace told them the story of Joseph and his coat of many colors. The way she delivered the story, the children might have been watching a movie or stage play because Grace took on every part, changing her voice to match each character.

On Sunday the entire clan headed to church. It had never before occurred to him how the sharing of a hymnal could be so exhilarating. He was actually glad when the minister announced that the congregation would sing all six verses of the hymn. Grace had a lovely voice and obviously knew the hymn. She sang with an expression of pure joy on her face—a face made even lovelier by the sunlight streaming in through the stained-glass windows next to her.

Jud had trouble concentrating on the sermon, so aware was he of the nearness of Grace. More than that, Jud found the experience of being back in the church of his childhood comforting. His talks with Grace's minister had continued—mainly through phone calls in the days following the engagement dinner. At Reverend Gibbs's urging, Jud was considering attending services again. And this weekend was the perfect place to start.

"You don't need the added pressure of having Grace and others question you about your return to formal services," the minister had advised. "Just go to services. Rediscover the feel of it, the power of the music and the words."

Talking with Tim Gibbs helped Jud focus on those matters that troubled him most. Slowly he had begun to put the past in perspective. For the first time since he'd been fired and discovered Charlotte's betrayal, he realized it had all brought him to a far better place in his personal and professional life. For one thing, he never would have met Grace.

But I've upset her. I can't think how. The article was perfect in every way—she said so herself. Nevertheless something I've done has upset her. Stop making excuses and think.

She seems to be over it.

You think so?

Yeah.

Think again.

Grace had mixed feelings about the weekend coming to an end. She and Jud were scheduled to leave soon after lunch—a full-fledged Sunday dinner complete with Connie's roast beef, oven-browned potatoes, and the last of the green beans, peas and corn frozen from the past summer's garden. The children proudly served up brownies, made from scratch using a recipe from Grace's grandmother.

"Grace, you have got to write down this recipe for me," Eva insisted. "She just threw it together," she explained to the others.

"We helped throw it together," her youngest protested.

"Yes, darling, but Mama isn't as talented as Auntie

Gracie, so I need to have it written down if you want to try it at home."

Auntie Gracie.

Grace blushed with pleasure. In less than two days Jud's family had taken her into their home and hearts. It felt as if she'd always known them. Her parents would absolutely love them. They were always drawn to people like Connie and Gus with no political agenda or pretense. In fact, throughout the weekend, she'd found herself fantasizing about what it might be like to be a permanent member of the family. Of course, that was a problem. It was Jud's family.

"And don't forget to give us your e-mail, Grace," Connie reminded her. "We want to stay in touch and if we rely on this one to give us information, we'll never hear of you again." She pinched Jud's cheek in a gesture that Grace understood only a mother could get away with.

"We'd better start heading back around two o'clock, if that's okay, Grace? I have some work to do tonight and there's always traffic coming back into the city after the weekend."

"Sure," Grace replied. "I'm packed already. I'll just help with the dishes."

"You will not," Connie announced. "This is an equal opportunity household and as such the men will take care of the dishes. Come on, Grace, let's take a walk before you have to spend the next couple of hours in that car. If my son is anything like his father there will be no stops unless the car is on fire."

The two women followed the path through the orchard to the north of the house. The day was gray and blustery, but it was refreshing to be outside and feel the rush of the wind on their faces.

"I'm so glad you came, Grace," Connie said.

"It's been a delightful weekend. I love your family, Connie. Your grandchildren are wonderful."

Connie laughed. "Well, that could be up for debate on any given day—especially the older ones." She hesitated. "Do you also love my son, Grace?" she asked quietly.

Grace was taken aback by the direct question, but Connie continued. "Because I've watched him all weekend and I'm old enough and experienced enough to know when my children are in love. Jud is in love with you."

"We really haven't known each other that long."

"As if that matters in today's world. Or yesterday's for that matter. On our second date Gus asked me to marry him. I was appalled when I found myself saying yes. You're the matchmaker, you know that when it's right time is not a factor."

Grace could hardly argue a point she had made many times herself. "We...that is...."

"I'm sorry. Is there someone else? I just assumed..."

"No. There's no one." No one but Jud. "We have some things to work out."

Connie grinned. "Aha! I told Gus that something had happened on the drive down. Unfinished business. Well, let's get you back up to the house and on your way so you can finish whatever that conversation might have been and get on with your life."

Grace didn't miss that she said "your life," not "lives," as if the two of them were one.

"Connie, Jud has told me how much you and Gus are looking forward to more grandchildren, especially from Jud, but you really can't push him toward marriage if he's not ready."

"He's ready," Connie said without hesitation. "He's made such changes in his life since meeting you. He came to church this morning—which he hasn't done in months, and he's become friends with Reverend Gibbs."

Grace tried not to reveal her surprise at this information. Jud friends with a minister—her minister? Surely Connie had misunderstood.

"Oh, he's definitely found the right woman in you." She interrupted before Grace could protest. "Grace, Jud has changed. I hear it in his phone calls, see it in his e-mails. He's more thoughtful, and I don't just mean considerate. He thinks things through in a way that he never did before."

"I suspect losing his job and the demotion had a great deal to do with that."

Connie nodded. "No doubt. But until you came into his life, he was only bitter about that. He couldn't seem to find his way past it. I've watched the way he was with you this weekend. It was enormously important to him that we like you and more to the point that you like us. For all the appearance he gives of being self-centered,

Jud is a family man—always has been. I do hope that your parents like him as much as we already adore you."

Grace knew that Connie was expecting an answer. Knew the answer she hoped to hear. "He definitely impressed them," she said, knowing it could be taken many ways.

"But?" Connie wasn't fooled. Then she slapped her palm to her forehead. "Of course, it's his job, right? Jud's a *good* reporter, Grace. He lost his way on that one story, but he's fair and he has integrity. He won't risk that again even for his career."

They had reached the house. Jud was loading the luggage into the car. The children were on the porch and came running to say goodbye as soon as they saw Grace, so there was no chance to respond to Connie. Grace counted her blessings.

After the hoopla of shared hugs and promises to e-mail and stay in touch, the enclosed space of the car seemed far too quiet. Jud and Grace made staccato stabs at small talk about the weekend while he navigated the roads to the highway, then both gave up and fell silent. It was really the first time they had been alone together since they'd arrived at his parents' home.

"Thank you for coming, Grace," Jud finally said. "You made the weekend very special, not just for Mom. The whole family loved you."

Grace couldn't understand why that statement made her eyes well up with tears. "They're really special, Jud. I'm so glad you asked me."

He took some time to digest and analyze that. "But?"

"No buts." She tried a laugh but it came out hollow.

Jud sighed and shifted in his seat as if trying to find a comfortable place. "Are you going to tell me what I've done that's upset you?"

So, here it was. The two of them had postponed this conversation for the whole of the weekend, allowing themselves to bask in the idyllic festivities of his mother's birthday and the family gathering. It was as if they'd spent a couple of days in Disneyland and now were coming back to face the real world.

Grace hesitated. She was reluctant to let go of the fantasy they had shared. Throughout the weekend she had allowed herself to fall into the role of Jud's girlfriend because he and his family made that so easy for her. They even seemed to believe—or wanted to believe—that it was who she was. Now, she understood that once they finished this conversation, that balloon would burst—perhaps forever.

"I like you, Jud," she began.

He actually grinned. She could see that he was still caught up in the magic of the weekend. "Oh, boy, I don't think I'm going to like this one bit."

"Please, be serious," she said testily. He was deliberately trying to dodge the issue.

"Okay. Just spit it out."

She took a deep breath. "It's about that evening at my parents' house. It's about a folder and some papers that you handled on my father's desk."

She watched him closely to see how he might form

his response. "And do not try to deny it, Jud. You went through my father's papers. The only question now is what you found and how you intend to use whatever you may have stolen that night."

"I explained this earlier, but again—for the record— I did not 'steal' anything."

"Ha!" It amazed her how quickly her anger flared.

"You think I deliberately faked a page from my editor so I could scope out your father's desk?"

"It hadn't occurred to me, but now that you bring it up, maybe so."

"What was I looking for?"

"Anything that would tie my father to Senator Mark Gordon is one guess."

"You cannot be serious," he replied, anger making his voice low and tight. "The rumor that Senator Gordon has been considering a switch in parties is not exactly a secret. It's been speculation in every political circle for weeks. I certainly didn't need to be looking for proof of that on your father's desk."

"But no one has had any hard evidence of how seriously to take that rumor—or did you find what you needed that night? Because it was right there in plain sight. You certainly didn't need to fake that business of papers falling to the floor."

"I'm telling you the truth, Grace. I got a page from Millie. Your father offered the library. I'm sitting there listening to Millie go on about nothing. Okay, not about nothing, about you and how it was going. I took in my surroundings. I won't deny that."

"And do you also sneak a peek into people's medicine cabinets when you are a guest in their home and use their bathroom?"

"That's not fair."

"But you don't deny that you viewed my father's personal property as fair game for your snooping around?"

"You're twisting my words. I sat at the desk. Millie was yammering on and on as she does. I got bored. I looked around. I stood and turned. The papers fell. By accident. End of story." He practically shouted it.

They said nothing for a long moment.

Finally she spoke. "Do you honestly expect me to believe that you weren't tempted? That you never even noticed the notes on the folder?"

"Obviously, you've already decided for yourself that I'm guilty. Denying anything would be pretty pointless."

Grace glanced at him, wanting so much to read in his eyes something that would put her doubts to rest once and for all. But Jud kept his eyes on the road and refused to look at her.

"Well, it's moot anyway. The fact remains that the only reason you've shown the slightest interest in me is because you thought I would be your portal to my father. I hate to spoil your grand ambitions, but Senator Gordon is going to stay right where he is. In fact, he's distancing himself from my father, which is a shame because they've always been good friends and worked well together in spite of party differences. But you don't care about the good those two men might have done for the country, do you? Your career takes precedence over all of that."

His hands gripped the steering wheel until his knuckles were white. He glanced her way. "I thought you were different."

"Don't you dare compare me to anyone else who might have hurt you in the past, Jud Marlowe. I did not use you. That shoe is on the other foot this time—your foot."

Neither of them said anything for several miles. Finally Grace couldn't stand the silence any longer. She actually felt a flicker of sympathy for him.

"So what will you do now?" Why on earth should she care?

"Don't ask me that," Jud said gruffly.

"Why not? There's still news in Gordon's decision not to switch parties."

"Don't patronize me, Grace."

"Suit yourself. But if you approach this in the right way for once instead of—"

"Oh, please enlighten me, Ms. Harrison, because you always do the right thing." He was shouting again and his voice dripped with sarcasm.

His anger was a spark for hers. "That can only be the right thing as God sees it," she shouted back. "There's right and wrong—black and white."

"I was under the impression that God also created a whole range of tones and tints to every color—besides black and white."

He swung the car onto her street and pulled up to her house with a squeal of the brakes.

"Pop the trunk. I'll get my stuff. There's no need for you to come in," she said, her voice almost choking as she fought against the threatening tears.

He did as she asked, waited until she was inside the house and then pulled away without another word.

Chapter Twelve

Mercifully, Bethany and Kim read her foul mood and asked no questions beyond, "How was the weekend?" when Grace arrived at the church office the following morning. Whether it was her puffy eyes and failed attempt to hide the circles that indicated a sleepless night, or the clipped "Fine" that she offered as a response, they got the message and said nothing more as she took her mail and messages and headed for her office.

Once inside, she closed the door and walked to the window. She leaned her forehead against the cool glass as she watched the rivulets of rain trickle down the pane.

I don't know what to do.

Grace pushed away from the window and forced her attention to the pile of messages from prospective candidates for the matchmaker program. "Some matchmaker I am," she said aloud as she flipped through the stack again and realized that she was looking for a message from Jud.

Preparations for the wedding of David and Suni took on whirlwind proportions as the date for Suni's parents to return home was moved up another week. Grace and Jud played their roles to perfection, never allowing their personal estrangement to intrude on the happiness of their friends. Fortunately David and Suni were so caught up in the activities surrounding the wedding that they barely noticed.

Jud was just as glad. The last thing he needed was Dave bugging him about Grace. His friend was sure to take her side, sure to assume that it was Jud who had somehow messed up. But the truth was in the weeks since he had gotten to know Grace, his career ambitions had taken on a new twist.

No longer was it simply a matter of reclaiming his place in the front lines of journalism. With Grace always on his mind he realized that he had begun to push harder because of her —because he knew that in order to be worthy of her, to stand a chance of building any kind of future with her, he needed to restore his reputation and turn failure into success. With no Gordon story, he was back to square one—both in his career and apparently with Grace.

What was I expecting? he thought late one night as he worked alone in the newsroom, gathering information for three deadlines that he'd let slide.

I thought she believed in me, in what I was doing to get back on track. She encouraged me.

Not to snoop through her father's private papers.

I didn't write anything down or use anything. Even Reverend Gibbs told me that was a good thing. At least it's a start. Okay, so it's more complex than that for Grace, and she's right about one thing. At the outset I was using her to get to her father. But Grace isn't going to applaud the fact that I almost took information but didn't. She thinks I'm better than that—or at least she did.

Jud paused in mid-keystroke and stared at the monitor, the only light in the room other than a small desk lamp. Then he typed *Career or Grace?*

He sat back and stared at the words for a long moment, then leaned forward and overwrote the word *or* with *and* which was, after all, what he really wanted.

Help me, he thought and froze. Exactly who was it he was asking to help?

He recalled the day he had interrupted Grace talking aloud, to herself he had thought. To God, she had told him and then had suggested that he did it as well, that everyone did it.

"Well, it's not exactly Paul on the road to Damascus," he muttered aloud, looking at the monitor where the cursor blinked repeatedly next to the word *and*. "But if You're trying to tell me something, I'm listening."

Silence. No sudden epiphany. Apparently God didn't talk back—at least not in a way Jud could hear.

"Okay, I could use a little help here." He practically shouted the words and smiled as they reverberated through the empty newsroom.

"Coming," a voice answered.

Jud almost fell off his chair.

The cleaning lady emerged from Millie's office, an overflowing wastebasket in one hand. "Be right there," she called across the expanse of cubicles.

Jud started to laugh. "You are seriously losing it, Marlowe." He shut down his computer and reached for his jacket.

"How can I help?" the cleaning lady asked, now standing in the entrance to his cube. She was around forty, and she had the most radiant smile.

Jud had watched the TV show where God appeared to the high school girl in various guises. He considered the possibility of that in reality and shook it off. "Nothing, thanks," he said. "Just thinking out loud."

The woman nodded sympathetically. "Big story?"

"Could've been," he replied, putting on his jacket.

"Political?"

"Yeah."

The woman paused and looked directly at him. "My mother—God rest her soul—would ask you if telling it could make a difference in the lives of ordinary people."

"My mother—very much alive—would ask if telling it would matter a week from now," he said and grinned.

The cleaning lady smiled back at him. "You'll find the answers to these questions."

"Perhaps."

She nodded and smiled with satisfaction. "Have a good evening, sir."

"And, you," he replied and left feeling better than he had in days.

The weather on the weekend of the wedding was perfect. Bulbs that had held their tight blooms for days now released them. Flowering trees seemed ready to explode in a riot of color. And yet, Grace couldn't seem to muster her usual delight that everything was going to be so perfect for David and Suni. She seemed incapable of thinking of anything other than that it was going to be a very long day, spent mostly in the company of Jud Marlowe.

The fact was that she missed him terribly. Missed their conversations. Missed his odd sense of humor. Missed considering the possibility that they might have a future together.

"Clearly, he doesn't share those feelings, so pull yourself together," she instructed her reflection in the mirror. "Get through the day and then move on."

"Okay, places everyone," Bethany shouted, clapping her hands to get the attention of the wedding party. "No, no, no!" she exclaimed as she pulled Suni from her position as bride. "This is the rehearsal. You can't be the bride. It's bad luck. Grace will play your part and Jud will be David." She placed her hands on her hips and tapped one high-heeled shoe impatiently as she looked down the long aisle to where David and Jud waited. "Well, switch places," she said with an exasperated sigh.

The men did as they were told and Bethany turned her attention to Grace.

"I really think you're taking this all too seriously," Grace said softly. "Relax. It's all going to be lovely."

Bethany looked at her as if she needed that assurance more than food itself. "Do you think so?"

"I do," Grace replied and was relieved to see Bethany's usual mischievous grin.

"Ah, save the 'I do' line for up there. I just hope that Jud can say it with as much conviction."

Before Grace could form a response, Bethany was gone, cueing the organist and clapping her hands to set the slow pace she wanted the bridesmaids to match on their way down the aisle. "And now the maid of honor."

Suni made everyone, even Bethany, laugh by doing a line dance step down the aisle.

"And the wedding march starts now," Bethany shouted up to the organist in the loft above the pews. "And here she comes, ladies and gentlemen, our bride of the hour. And one-pause-two-pause…"

Reverend Gibbs cleared his throat and glanced at his watch. "And so it goes," he called and motioned for the organist to cut the music short as everyone gathered round the altar.

"Ambassador and Mrs. Ashraff, take your place there in the front row. Perfect." Bethany scurried forward. "Now Grace, this is when you will straighten Suni's train—that is, after handing your bouquet to the closest bridesmaid, of course."

"Got it," Grace replied, grinning at Suni, who was rolling her eyes. Grace turned her attention back to the minister and found herself standing not two feet from

Jud, who was watching her with that infuriatingly engaging grin.

The minister opened the small black book he was holding and again cleared his throat. "Dearly beloved, we are blah...blah...blah..." He slowly turned pages as he continued actually saying, "Blah, blah, blah."

Grace felt a fit of giggles coming on as she imagined Bethany steaming away behind her. Suni pretended to sneeze but there was no doubt that she, too, was about to explode into laughter. David was biting his lip to keep from grinning. Only Jud set his laughter free.

Reverend Gibbs grinned. "Clearly tomorrow, I will be a bit more erudite," he said with a smile.

"One can hope," Bethany muttered and this time everyone did laugh.

"Okay, we've come to the business of rings. David and Suni, you will want to watch this closely. Jud, please take Grace's hand."

The minister continued his lesson of the rings, but Grace was aware of nothing but Jud's hand holding hers and miming the placing of the ring on her finger.

"Grace?"

She blinked and pulled her eyes away from Jud's face. Everyone was looking at her. "Sorry," she murmured and quickly pulled her hand free of Jud's.

"Now it's your turn," the minister said gently. "Take Jud's hand. That's right." He turned his attention to Suni, instructing her on what to do if by some misfortune she dropped the ring while Grace stood there holding Jud's hand and felt his thumb stroking her palm as he gazed down at her.

"And then there's the usual wrap-up—if anyone present knows any reason why this man and this woman should not be joined in holy matrimony, blah, blah, blah."

Because my father doesn't think I can trust him? Is that enough to let him go? Grace thought as she searched Jud's face for some sign that she was wrong. Because I convinced myself that I meant more to him than just a story. Because...

"...kiss the bride."

Before Grace could think what was happening Jud leaned in and placed his lips on hers. Around her, through the fog of her disbelief that he was actually kissing her, she heard the cheers and applause of her friends. His mouth was warm and gentle. She could easily pull away, but no. She kissed him back.

The organist struck up the postlude as she and Jud pulled a fraction of an inch away from each other, both obviously stunned by what had just happened.

"Well," said Reverend Gibbs, "usually we skip that specific piece of the rehearsal."

He grinned at Grace. This was her minister—her boss! She felt her cheeks flame to a rosy glow, then grabbed Jud's arm and propelled him halfway up the aisle. Bethany was waiting for them with a huge knowing grin spread across her wide mouth.

"That was fun," Jud announced, wrapping one arm around Grace's shoulders and pulling her close. "But

David's a little slow. Maybe we should go through that last bit again?"

"I think I got it, pal," David said and pulled Suni into his arms and kissed her to prove his point.

"I hate to break this up," the minister said, "but we have choir rehearsal starting in a few minutes and I believe you are all expected at the rehearsal dinner?"

Immediately, Bethany was back in charge, herding them all toward the door with last-minute reminders of appointments and times for the following day. Grace watched as Jud hung back and spoke with Reverend Gibbs. The conversation was obviously serious and when they parted, the minister gave Jud a brief hug.

David's parents hosted the dinner at a small Italian restaurant that they had taken over for the evening in Old Alexandria. The place was packed by the time the wedding party arrived. The music and conversation were loud, making it impossible for Grace and Jud to talk. Grace said a prayer of thanks for found blessings. The last thing she wanted to do was analyze that kiss.

But after all the introductions of out-of-town guests and toasts from friends and family, she found herself alone with Jud for the first time all evening. People were starting to leave and she was reclaiming her coat from the coat check when he reached past her and took the coat from the attendant.

He held it out for her. She saw no way to refuse his kindness and so turned and slipped her arms through the sleeves. He brought the coat to rest on her shoulders and then allowed his hands to linger there a moment longer before releasing her. "May I see you home?"

"I don't think—"

"Stop thinking," he interrupted with a decided edge, before adding more gently, "Tomorrow's going to be a special day for our friends. I just hoped that we could maybe clear the air tonight."

He was right, of course. Even in their euphoria, David and Suni had both begun to notice the strain, had both tried to help, and had both failed. "Okay," she agreed. "Walk with me to the metro."

Once they had said their goodbyes and Grace had endured the gleeful Bethany's whisper encouragement to "go for it," they were both silent for the first several blocks. Then Jud took a deep breath.

"Grace, I'm just going to say it. No guts, no glory."

"Say what?" Her heart beat faster.

"I'm in love with you, Grace Harrison."

Grace stopped dead in her tracks. Jud walked on for a couple of yards, then retraced his steps until he was standing very close to her. "I'm in love with you and, frankly, it's driving me nuts."

"What about your career?"

He stared at her, his face in shadow so that she couldn't read it. "What?"

"Your career."

Jud shook his head as if to clear cobwebs. "What are you talking about? What has my career got to do with telling you that I love you? Look, Grace, if you don't have feelings for me just say so. I'm a grown man. I can take it. I don't need you to do let me down easy."

"It's not that simple."

"Do you love me or not?"

"I could," she admitted but it came out as part of the heat of the moment.

"But?" His jaw was set, his shoulders hunched as he shoved his fists into his coat pockets.

Grace took a breath, trying to calm herself and think. "Surely you can see how impossible the idea of us together is. I mean, you're a reporter and I'm..."

"Don't you dare fall back on 'daughter of Senator Harrison' as an excuse," he said between gritted teeth. "You've spent most of your adult life distancing yourself from that label and I'm sure not going to let you pull it out now just because it's convenient."

It was exactly what she had been going to do. She looked for some other path. "Fine. How about the fact that you've never denied that you used me to gather information about my father and perhaps Senator Gordon? How can people in love do things like that? Love has to carry an element of trust."

He started to say something but she wasn't finished. "And don't tell me that you weren't in love with me then. We're talking about ethics and fundamental decency here."

"If I changed, then you could admit you love me?"

"Oh, Jud, you know that never works. I don't want to change you."

"What if I told you that I've already changed—because of you, because of what I've learned about myself since meeting you?"

"You're not listening," she said miserably. "What I'm saying is that love between us has no future."

"Not if you don't believe in us," he said. He paced back and forth, trying hard to get his temper under control. "So where do we go from here?"

Grace sat on a park bench with a weary sigh. She had wanted so much not to say what she knew she must. "We get through tomorrow and then go our separate ways. We'll run into each other because we are both friends with David and Suni, but over time, we'll find a way to be just that—people who share mutual friends and nothing more."

He sat next to her, but on the edge of the bench as if at any moment he might take off running. "That's it? You won't even give me—us—a chance?"

She took a long moment to consider that. "You must find your own answers, Jud. Whether it's your work or your faith or your relationship with me or anything else."

"I can get there, Grace, with your help." He sat next to her and took her hands in his.

She shook her head slowly and looked down at their entwined hands. "It isn't my help you need, Jud." She looked up at him, ready for his objections, but the shuttered expression she had come to know so well whenever the subject of God came up was missing. She touched his cheek. "Perhaps if we had met under other circumstances…" She stood, then bent and kissed the top of his head. "I'll see you tomorrow."

* * *

The church was decorated with huge sprays of spring blossoms. The guests filled the pews. David and Jud, in beautifully fitted tuxedos, waited with the minister at the front of the sanctuary. Four bridesmaids in elegant black satin gowns and groomsmen in tuxedos had already made their way down the aisle. Grace was wearing a soft blue-gray silk gown that did wonders for her flawless skin and dark hair. Bethany had done her hair and makeup and even Grace had to agree that the result was nothing short of stunning. She stood at the back of the church, feeling beautiful and confident as she awaited Bethany's cue.

"Smile," Bethany ordered as she sent Grace on her way.

Every eye was on her as she took the long slow walk toward the altar, but the only person she was aware of was Jud. Her confidence wavered. He was staring at her with such undisguised longing that she blushed. At first she dealt with it by doing what Bethany referred to as her version of Princess Diana's "Shy Di" look—head slightly lowered but eyes wide and watching.

"Smile," Bethany hissed when Grace was only a few steps down the aisle. Grace forced a smile and nodded to her parents seated about midway back on the bride's side of the aisle. On the other side of the aisle sat Jud's parents. Connie was smiling at her through misty eyes. Then Grace made the mistake of looking ahead, at Jud. David also looked at Grace and then said something to Jud, who smiled.

Grace forced herself to relax and focus on the ceremony. Perhaps somehow, someday, it could all work out for them. Perhaps there was a chance they could have a future after all.

She had reached the altar, then Jud and David stepped forward. Everyone turned toward the back of the church as the organist struck up "The Wedding March," and Suni floated down the aisle in a gown of white satin on the arm of her beaming father.

Grace couldn't concentrate on the ceremony. Her mind was filled with images of Jud. When Reverend Gibbs finally introduced the new Mr. and Mrs. Forrester, the congregation broke into spontaneous applause. Grace released her breath and bent to straighten Suni's train as David and Suni headed back up the aisle.

When she stood, there was Jud, offering his arm and smiling broadly. She smiled back and cupped her hand in the crook of his arm, trying not to dwell on the hard muscle, or recall how it had felt to be held in those strong arms. All the way up the aisle, he talked to her while never losing his broad smile.

"You look amazing, Grace. Beautiful. Radiant. Suni definitely finished a poor second today."

"Stop that," Grace muttered while smiling and nodding at the guests as they passed, but she couldn't deny that her heart swelled with delight at his compliments.

"Okay, I admit it. You could be wearing a burlap sack and still be the most beautiful woman in the room." He glanced down at her for a moment and added, "At least in my eyes."

And then she saw in his eyes that it was all an act—
the smiles, the compliments, the pretense that everything was all right.

He was as miserable as she was.

Chapter Thirteen

After David and Suni had basked in the toasts and good wishes of all their guests, enjoyed their wedding dinner and cut the cake, Jud clicked a spoon against his glass and the hall fell silent.

"To my best friend, David, and my new friend, Suni, for showing us all that there are matches that truly are made in heaven, and may those of us still searching be as fortunate as they were in the hunt for lifelong happiness." He raised his glass to the couple but his eyes were once again on Grace.

To her great relief, it was Bethany who caught the bouquet as the happy couple prepared to leave for their honeymoon. The last thing she needed was for Bethany and Kim to take that toast plus the bouquet and declare it a sign from God that she and Jud were meant for each other.

How I wish that could be true.

Maybe someday. If only he would come to that decision on his own—to accept Your plan for his life.

* * *

It had taken all of his willpower to get through the wedding. Everything about it drove Jud crazy—David's happiness, the beaming parents, the gushing guests. But what was nearly his undoing was Grace. The moment he saw her framed in the doorway at the rear of the church, he thought his heart would stop. Every step that brought her closer was excruciating. When she reached the altar and turned away from him to take her place as maid of honor, he realized that for a moment he had been about to step forward and take her hand.

Determined not to allow his melancholia in any way affect David and Suni's happiness, he forced himself to play the charming best man. He complimented the mothers on their gowns. He flirted with the bridesmaids. He organized the groomsmen to decorate David's car. He made the expected toast. He smiled, laughed, ate cake, threw rice and all the while, he watched Grace.

He was thinking of asking to see her home when he saw her preparing to leave with Bethany and her fiancé.

What more is there to say? he asked himself. How can I make her understand that I'm not the same man she met that day at the Capitol? That knowing her has led me to new understanding of myself?

After watching Grace leave, Jud decided to grab a change of clothes from his car and head back to the newsroom. He had a number of pieces in the works, stories that Millie would expect to be completed by Monday. Routine assignments about various city committees and panels.

Routine is good, he thought.

The large newsroom was mostly empty and lit only by the occasional lamp where a few reporters worked the phones or hammered out a story. Jud nodded to a couple of them as he walked the length of the room to his desk. He opened his article on the Parks Commission follow up and added the final paragraph. Then he found his notes on the plans for a festival to celebrate the history and traditions of the city and forced himself to focus.

One by one, the other journalists left. The room grew darker. Jud leaned back in his battered swivel chair and closed his eyes. His cell phone rang.

"Marlowe, that you?" There was no mistaking the raspy voice of his mentor and former editor, Hal Davis.

"What's up?"

"Sorry it's so late. I just called to see how things are going," Hal said. "Millie tells me she gave you a chance to go big-time with the connection you made to Harrison through his daughter."

"There's no story, Hal."

"Really? What about Gordon and the whole party switch thing?"

"Gordon already made it crystal clear several weeks ago that he could never go against his fundamental belief in the principles of his own party," Jud said impatiently. "There's nothing new there."

"Of course, that doesn't need to mean there's no story. Ever think about what he hoped to accomplish by switching in the first place?"

"Balance of power shift?"

"It's not always about power, Jud."

Jud slammed his chair forward, on full alert now. Hal was right. He'd been looking at this from the wrong angle. "What do you think it's about?" he asked his mentor.

"Doesn't matter what I think. You need to ask the man himself. Ask both of them, Gordon and Harrison. You're the perfect one to do it."

Jud's excitement was short-lived. Why on earth would either senator give him the time of day? He told Hal about Harrison's belief that he'd stolen information from his desk.

"Set up a meeting with Harrison," Hal advised. "Apologize. Convince him you were tempted but didn't act on it. Then bring Gordon into it. The key is to get these guys talking again."

Hal had a point. At the moment the two senators were making every effort to maintain a political distance from each other. Each was working overtime to demonstrate loyalty to his own party.

"Don't sit on this. You've got a real chance to do something good with this one." Jud could almost see Hal smile. "Give Millie my best and when the story breaks, tell her she owes me."

It took Jud a few minutes to realize what his former boss had just handed him. He opened a new file and keyed in points he needed to make with Grace's father. He considered asking Tim Gibbs to attend the meeting with him.

Whatever it takes to make him understand, he thought.

And Grace?

He stopped in mid-keystroke. Grace. Could she forgive him for having been tempted in the first place?

Jud buried his head in his hands.

Help me. I don't know what to do.

The silence inside his head was deafening.

What about Hal's comment about the chance to do good?

Jud replayed Hal's words, understanding the reference to making good. That was Hal's way of saying that this was his break. But doing good?

Jud paused and looked at his monitor for a long moment. "Maybe what Hal meant was…" he said softly, as the germ of an idea took form, an idea he would have considered bizarre just a few months earlier—before he met Grace.

What if Harrison and Gordon worked together in spite of their differences?

"Oh, sure," Jud said sarcastically. "I'll just call up both senators and tell them I have this bright idea. They'll probably invite me up to the Hill to talk it through."

But he pulled out his PalmPilot and found the number for Harrison's senate office. He'd call first thing Monday morning.

Two days after the wedding, Grace came home and heard her father and Ken in the library discussing Jud.

"You are telling me that Marlowe had the audacity to contact my office directly?" her father shouted. "After what he did?"

"He called and made an appointment," Ken replied.

"And you took it?"

Grace lingered at the foot of the stairs. On the one hand, she didn't want to know. On the other, she had to know. Her father was tapping his pen on the desk, a habit when he was thinking through strategy in a situation that posed a potential threat to his work.

"Riley, what if Marlowe has decided to go ahead with the story about Gordon toying with the idea of a party switch?" Ken asked. "If he does..."

"I know," the senator said with a weary sigh. He continued tapping the pen in the silence that followed.

"I hate to bring this up, but perhaps Grace..."

"No," her father replied firmly. "We are not involving my daughter."

"But, Senator, this thing could really come back on you if we aren't careful."

The tapping of the pen stopped. "The question is, what's he got?"

"About a week ago he had lunch with a former senior member of Gordon's staff. Maybe she gave him something."

"Who?"

"Elaine Bennett."

Grace's heart sank. She had introduced Jud to Elaine, suggested the two of them might hit it off, even encouraged Jud to call her. She heard her father release a heavy sigh, a sigh filled with all the frustration of long days and nights trying to put something together that could benefit all Americans.

"What do you want me to do?" Ken asked quietly.

"Nothing," her father replied. "The man works for Millie. She'd run a story indicting her grandmother if she thought it would sell papers. It was probably her idea to have him contact the office."

"I'm pretty sure that Millie knows nothing about Marlowe's call," Ken said. "She's had Grady Hunter from her news desk on the party switch story, but Hunter found nothing. Like every other media outlet in the beltway, Millie has pretty much moved on to other news."

"Really? Hunter? He must have been the one who contacted Gordon. I thought it was Jud." The tapping of the pen stopped. "I may have misjudged the boy," he said more to himself than to Ken.

Grace and her mother were relaxing in the family room when the doorbell rang around ten o'clock a week later. They had both changed into pajamas and robes. Grace had washed her hair and crunched it with her fingers to encourage some wave and body. Soothing classical music played in the background as she caught up on some church work and her mother worked on her needlepoint.

"Who on earth could be calling at this hour?" Grace asked. Her mother didn't seem the least bit surprised by a late-night visitor.

"Your father is expecting some guests," Catherine replied and went back to her needlework. "That's probably Mark Gordon."

"At this hour?"

"Mary, answer the door," her father called from the library. "I'm on the phone."

Their housekeeper had already left for the day, so Grace put aside her work and tightened the sash on her robe. The bell chimed again and her mother looked up at her. "Are you going to answer it?"

Suddenly it dawned on Grace why her parents wouldn't be surprised at a caller at this hour. If Senator Gordon was coming to the house, this had to be wonderful news for her father. She swung the door wide and smiled. "Senator—"

Jud grinned. "He's on his way," he said and waited politely for her to invite him inside.

"Marlowe?"

Grace turned at the sound of her father's booming voice. The senator offered him a firm handshake as Jud stepped inside. The demeanor of both men was solemn as Jud followed her father across the hall. "Right on time," he commented and ushered him into the library. "Gracie, just send Senator Gordon in when he gets here." He didn't wait for a response, just closed the door.

Not a minute later, she heard a car pull up outside. She looked through the side window next to the door and saw Elijah waving to Senator Mark Gordon before pulling away. She opened the door. "Hello, Senator," she said politely.

The senator kissed her cheek as he entered the foyer. "Sorry to disturb your evening, Grace. Hello, Catherine," he added when Grace's mother stepped into the foyer.

"I'll make some coffee," she said. "You take yours black, don't you, Mark?" Senator Gordon nodded. Grace's mother turned to her. "And Jud?"

"Black," Grace replied automatically.

"Lovely," Catherine said as she headed for the kitchen. "No fuss."

"They're in the library," Grace said, realizing that Senator Gordon hadn't been surprised at the mention of Jud. "But you already knew that."

Gordon smiled and patted her on the shoulder. "It's going to be all right, Grace. That's some young man you've found for yourself. Impressive."

Grace felt as if everyone, including Jud, was in on something that indirectly involved her. She headed straight for the kitchen.

"Okay, what's going on?"

"Your father and Mark plan to make an important announcement tomorrow at a joint press conference."

"I thought Senator Gordon had changed his mind about switching parties."

Catherine shrugged.

"And Jud is involved how?"

"Well, first he called your father and apologized for—well, his almost indiscretion when it came to items on your father's desk."

Catherine seemed inclined to savor that for a moment. Grace tried patience but it didn't last. "He apologized? And?"

"Then he mentioned that he should have realized that the real story lay in the ability and determination of these two very different men to look past their personal philosophical differences and truly work together. I thought that was beautifully put."

Grace tried hard to digest what she was hearing. "You're saying that Jud got Dad and Senator Gordon together?"

Catherine smiled as she leaned against the counter waiting for the coffee to drip through the system. "In a manner of speaking. He raised the question—could two such powerful men work together for the greater good without one of them having to abandon his principles and switch parties? Your father and Mark took matters from there."

"You're saying that Jud did this? Orchestrated this meeting tonight?"

"Not exactly, although I suppose you could say that he set things in motion. It seems that falling in love with you has its rewards. He told your father that loving you had made him look at things differently—at his career differently."

Grace's head was spinning.

"Mom, this is the same man who snooped around in Dad's personal papers right under our noses when we had been kind enough to invite him to dinner."

Catherine waved her hand in a gesture of dismissal and turned to place mugs on a tray. "He explained that."

"To Dad's satisfaction?"

"He brought Reverend Gibbs with him."

"Our minister?" This was beyond bizarre.

"Well, I believe that he's now Jud's minister as well. He knows everything. So there you have it."

Grace was ready to scream, "No! I don't have it at all." Instead she said tightly, "Mom, what is going on in there?"

"Mark and your father have decided to announce a major cooperative effort to enact key legislation on a number of issues. I think they're hammering out a press release now, which is, of course, why Jud is here."

Her mother handed her the tray. "Take this in and see for yourself. Honestly, dear, you do need to cut that young man some slack. Apparently, he's working very hard to live up to your expectations and high standards. At least that was part of what he told your father."

Grace balanced the tray on a side table and tapped lightly. Her father opened the door, but all three men continued to focus on their discussion.

"What else, Jud?" Senator Gordon asked, looking quite relaxed and calm as he sat in a one of the two wing-backed chairs facing her father's desk.

Jud sat at the desk, his fingers flying over the keyboard of her father's computer. He paused, glanced up at Grace, smiled and then turned his attention back to the monitor. "What about your constituents at home? How will they see this, especially after all the speculation about your going over to the other side?"

Grace's father handed out mugs of coffee and laughed. "Great question, Jud. Have you got an answer for that one, Mark?"

Senator Gordon took a sip of his coffee, pausing to gather his thoughts. Then he launched into a long-winded response, one he had clearly spent some time putting together. Jud concentrated on keying in every word.

"I'll just leave this here," Grace said quietly as she set the tray and pot of coffee on a sideboard.

"No, don't say it that way," her father interrupted Senator Gordon. "You want something simple and straightforward. Too much sounds like you're trying to rationalize. Gracie, why should his supporters back home be okay with our joining forces?"

"Hopefully because you're both doing this for them and not in spite of them," Grace replied, her attention so focused on Jud that she was hardly aware she'd spoken.

All three men looked up at her. Her father wrapped his arm around her shoulders and hugged her. "That's my girl."

Jud tapped the delete key to erase what Senator Gordon had dictated and then looked at Grace. "Can you say that again?"

"I..." All of them were staring at her, big smiles on their faces. Suddenly she was aware that she was wearing pajamas and a robe. Too late now, she thought. They've already seen me. She quickly refocused on Jud's request. "Hopefully," she began.

"Scratch the 'hopefully,'" Gordon said quietly as Jud nodded and typed. "We're doing this for the people, not in spite of them," he finished and beamed at Grace.

"Is Jud writing your announcement?" Grace asked. As weird as that seemed it was the only possible explanation.

The men laughed.

"Hardly," her father replied. "Mark and I are giving him an exclusive interview which will run in tomorrow's paper before the press conference."

"*Before* the press conference?"

Her father grinned. "A new twist. Every time anyone in this town calls a press conference, the press already know all the answers, so why not go ahead and break the news and then use the press conference as it was intended—to answer questions?"

"It's really quite brilliant, don't you think?" Senator Gordon asked.

Grace looked at Jud. "You came up with this idea?"

"Well, not exactly. I just offered to help if I could." He shrugged and flashed that infuriatingly charming grin of his.

"He's being modest, Grace."

"I'm also on a deadline. Millie's holding page one," he reminded them. He looked from the monitor to Grace, obviously torn between the story and wanting to be with her. "Could I call you tomorrow, maybe after you've had a chance to read the paper?"

Grace nodded and backed toward the open door.

"Okay. Sure. I'll say good-night then." She smiled at Senator Gordon and kissed her father's cheek, but she was looking at Jud as she left the room and quietly closed the door.

The three men worked late into the night. Around midnight, Catherine kissed Grace's forehead and suggested they both go to bed.

"You go on. I'll be up in a bit," Grace said, even though she was fighting to keep her eyes open.

"It's all going to work out, Grace. He's done the right thing and more."

"I just want to finish this chapter," Grace said, indicating the book that she'd barely read since the doorbell first rang hours earlier.

Catherine smiled. "Whatever you say, dear."

Alone, Grace put all pretense of reading aside and tried to understand how things had changed so dramatically in the past few hours. The very idea of Jud in there with her father and Senator Gordon was mindboggling. But for everything that might mean for his career and his relationship with her father, Grace couldn't help but wonder what this meant for her.

"I really have to send this now if it's going to make the morning edition," Jud told the senators. It was just after two o'clock in the morning and Harrison and Gordon were still picking the announcement apart, looking for any pitfalls that they might need to address at the press conference.

"Okay?" Harrison asked Gordon.

"Works for me," Gordon replied and extended his hand to Riley Harrison.

"Oh, where's a photographer when you need one," Harrison said with a laugh as he took his friend's hand and pulled him into a bear hug.

"I'm sending this," Jud said as a last warning.

The senators looked his way and nodded. Jud pressed the send key.

"We'd better get some sleep," Gordon said, gathering his briefcase and coat. "Jud, would you care to share a cab?"

"Thank you, sir," Jud replied.

Grace's father opened the door and across the hall the light of a single lamp fell on a sleeping Grace.

"Excuse me a moment. I'll be right there," Jud said and crossed the hall to where Grace slept.

He brushed a lock of hair away from her eyes. She stirred but didn't wake. He pulled the afghan higher around her shoulders. "Be sure you read *both* stories tomorrow, Gracie," he whispered as he bent and kissed her slightly parted lips.

It wasn't hard to spot the headline on the stacks of *Washington Today* as Grace headed for the metro the following morning. Elijah had driven her father to his office to prepare for the press conference and the senator had taken their home-delivered copy of the paper with him. Grace picked up a copy and absently dropped her money on the newsstand counter as she looked first at the large file photo of her father and a smiling Senator Gordon and then at the byline for the article—Jud Marlowe.

As she waited for the train, she scanned the story, smiling when she saw the quote that she had provided. She was impressed that Jud had probed deeper than the sound bite she had offered. In the finished article Gordon's rationale made the cooperative effort sound more than a little heroic and most definitely patriotic.

On the train ride, she alternated between rereading the article and staring out the window even after the train had rumbled underground on its way into the city.

I'm confused. What does this mean?

She had no answer. Resigned, Grace turned her attention back to the newspaper, half-heartedly flipping through the sections, and then stopping when she came to the Lifestyle section. There was a photo of Suni and David at their wedding. The headline read "Happily Ever After? Is the Fairy Tale Ending for Real?"

She pulled her glasses into place and prepared to scan the article.

For David and Suni Forrester (née Ashraff), the fairy-tale ending actually began this past Saturday in a wedding ceremony and celebration that absolutely throbbed with omens of happily ever after. The groom was handsome; the bride, a veritable princess. The parents on both sides of the aisle were beaming with pride and joy. And yet, something was missing. This reporter decided he, too, wanted a happily ever after and is determined to construct his own fairy-tale ending.

Grace's mouth tightened. She forced herself to reserve judgment until she had read the entire thing, however upsetting it was going to be.

Once upon a time, a reporter had, in the course of following the love story of David and Suni, found his own true love. In the beginning his chances for finding what his friends had found seemed impossible. For he had not only fallen in love with a princess—he had fallen in love with the daughter of one of the most powerful men in the kingdom. The object of his dreams was also a professional matchmaker. Surely, she knew how to find her own true love. She had done it for others with great success. And why would she be interested in someone like him?

But the matchmaker always saw the basic goodness to be found in every person, even in this reporter. He felt a glimmer of hope, but quickly dashed any such thoughts. He knew better than to dare hope that they might have a future. After all, he'd seen a side of the world that she hadn't. He'd spent his adult life writing stories about real people who were not always kind and good, who would not always make the best choice if money or success were at stake. He knew that deep down he could be one of those people.

The train stopped at her station, but Grace was so engrossed that she hardly noticed. She hurried on to finish the article.

She worked in a church and her faith was the basis for everything she did. He had pretty much abandoned the church and his own religious upbringing as irrelevant. It was her job to find the best in people and his to find the worst, because it's the worst that sells newspapers and boosts ratings for broadcast news.

One day she invited him to dinner at her powerful father's castle. The reporter, not yet realizing that he was falling in love with the matchmaker, was thrilled. He very much wanted to write a story about the powerful father, but not just any story—a story that would get the reporter noticed by his editor.

And, just as he had dreamed, that night at dinner in the castle, the reporter found himself sitting in front of information that he could probably use to write that story. Right there under his nose. He was tempted, of course.

But then a strange thing happened. As soon as the reporter started touching the papers and files that could lead to what he needed, he realized what he was doing. He was stealing. Would he allow himself to stoop to the depths of common thievery to achieve success?

The reporter looked up and saw the woman he loved watching him, with great disappointment clouding her blue eyes. And the reporter realized that he didn't like that. He left the castle as quickly as he could.

The reporter remembered that the matchmaker had once told him that God guides the actions of every person who seeks His help. The reporter had laughed at her naiveté, but he wasn't laughing now. He was listening.

But was the princess still listening?

MATCHMAKER, MATCHMAKER, WILL YOU MARRY ME?

To be continued...

Grace stared at the words. She took off her glasses, cleaned them and stared at the words again.

Jud had actually proposed to her in the paper.

Chapter Fourteen

Realizing that she had gone well beyond her destination, Grace used her cell phone to call her father's car service. If Elijah was still near the Senate office building, he was near enough to swing around and pick her up. That settled, she called the church.

"Kim, is Tim in yet?"

"Right here. Did you see Jud's article?"

"Yes. Please put Tim on. I need to speak with him."

"Grace?" the reverend answered.

"My mom said that Jud told you everything that happened the night of the engagement party. Is it true?"

"Yes."

"He came to you that same night?"

"He did. We met in my office and we talked, then a little later we prayed together."

"And you've met other times?"

"We talk two or three times a week. That young man has been carrying around a great deal of anger and guilt. He was more than relieved to be able to put it down. Not to mention a little surprised that doing so could be as simple as letting God help."

"But—"

"Grace, I believe that Jud's return to his faith is genuine. I also believe that God used you as his instrument to make that happen."

Grace was speechless.

"Grace, are you there?"

"I don't know what to say."

Tim laughed. "Say 'yes,' my dear."

Grace gathered her things and exited the train at the next stop. She ran up the escalator to the street just as Elijah pulled to a stop several yards past her and threw the car into reverse.

"You gonna do it?" he asked when she had gotten in and closed the door.

"Thanks for picking me up," she said, ignoring his question although it was certainly the only question on her mind at the moment.

"I wouldn't have wanted to miss this," he replied.

They rode in silence for a few blocks. Elijah watched her in the rearview mirror. She stared out the window and pretended not to notice.

"You gonna tell me where you want to go?"

"I…I really don't know," she said softly.

"Well, I do. You've got to settle this thing once and for all. The man should be at his office, shouldn't he?"

"Maybe. Maybe he's on an assignment."

"Maybe one day the Washington Monument will

stand on its point for a while. Let's start with the newspaper." He hurtled across town at breakneck speed, pulled up to the unimpressive building that housed the offices of *Washington Today.* "You go on up there. I'll wait."

"I don't know what to say," Grace faltered.

"Do you love him?"

"Yes, but..."

"There's no buts if you love him, Gracie. The man's put his heart out there for the world to see. He must be head over heels for you to take a risk like that."

Grace smiled and then she started to laugh. "Wonder what he'd do if I said no?"

Elijah rolled his eyes. "What floor are they on? I'm asking so I can alert security to watch for a man jumping out the window."

When Grace strode into the lobby the security guard and receptionist recognized her at once. "Hello, Ms. Harrison," the receptionist said nervously, looking up from a copy of Jud's Lifestyle story. "Fourteenth floor. Left, off the elevator."

Grace nodded and stepped into the elevator the security guard was holding open for her. "Hope you say yes," he said as the doors slid shut.

Millie Peterson had sprung for an impressive breakfast spread to celebrate Jud's victory in getting the exclusive on the groundbreaking legislative effort between two former adversaries. "A New Dawn for Partisan Politics," the bold headline had declared. But his coworkers, especially the females, were far more interested in his little fairy tale on the Lifestyle page.

"What do you think will happen?" he heard one woman whisper to her cohorts as they smeared cream cheese on bagels and helped themselves to paper cups filled with freshly squeezed orange juice.

"Well, she has to say yes, don't you think? I mean, look at him. He's gorgeous. She'd have to be brain-dead to turn that down."

From your mouth to God's ears, Jud thought as he smiled at them on his way to his cubicle.

"Whoa! Don't look now, pal, but she's here," the guy across from him whispered.

Grace paused in the doorway, looked around and then spotted Jud.

Jud thought his heart would either stop altogether or pound its way right through the wall of his chest as he watched her walk the length of the room. She was carrying the newspaper, tapping it lightly against her thigh as she walked. She looked neither left nor right. Jud was aware that editors had come to the doors of their offices to see what might happen next.

"She hates publicity," he heard someone mutter.

"Yeah, he broke that rule, big-time," another agreed.

Jud swallowed hard. He tried to read her expression. He mentally berated himself for his impetuousness. Last night with the deadline looming it had seemed a wonderful idea—the story on page one with her father's blessing and then the proposal to cap it off. His fingers had flown over the keyboard. He'd never in his life had two such different articles come together so perfectly. Millie hadn't made a single change to either one. She was a romantic at heart.

He glanced over at Millie just as Grace turned the last corner of the maze that would bring her to his cubicle. Millie's expression was very easy to read. It said, "You're on your own now, kid."

"Hello," Grace said quietly as if no one in the room was even aware of her presence.

"Hi." Jud glanced down at his desk chair. "Why don't you take this and I can..."

His coworker across the aisle stood, rolled his own desk chair toward Jud's cubicle and then went to refill his coffee.

"I thought we should talk," Grace said, not taking either seat. "Preferably in private."

There was a definite muffled, but audible, groan throughout the newsroom.

"Look, Grace, I..."

Millie stepped forward. "Hello, Grace. Nice to see you again. Jud, I can send Hunter to cover the press conference. You go ahead. Take all the time you need." She smiled at Grace and then gave the rest of the newsroom a look that sent them scurrying back inside their offices and cubicles.

Grace smiled. "Thank you. Nice to see you, too, Millie." She turned her attention back to Jud.

"I'll just get my jacket," he said unnecessarily, having already slung it over his shoulder.

Grace led the way, smiling and nodding at those who dared to look up at her as they left.

There were three other people on the elevator, so they both stood looking up at the lights signaling the passing floors until they came to the lobby. Jud didn't miss the way the security guard and receptionist looked at Grace, nor the way she simply smiled at them. Outside he had to quicken his step to keep up with her as she headed for the curb.

"Where are we going?"

"That's your decision," she said as Elijah emerged from the car and held the door for her.

"My decision? I don't even know what's going on here," he shouted in exasperation.

Elijah frowned and waited for Jud to climb in next to Grace. "I'll give you two a minute," he said, reaching in through the driver's side window to retrieve his coffee and then perching himself on the hood.

"Look, Grace, I know you hate being in the papers and everything, but…"

She held up the newspaper. "Is this your idea of a proper proposal of marriage, Jud Marlowe?" She didn't wait for an answer, just shook her head slowly and kept talking. "I knew that I should have made sure you got the full program. I mean you barely got the rudiments to get started. And this proves it."

"I have no idea what you're talking about," Jud said hotly. "This is serious. I want to marry you. I want us to…"

Grace placed her fingers over his lips. "Stop right

there. Jud, a woman wants romance and magic when it comes to a proposal of marriage."

"I thought this *was* romantic," he replied, unable to disguise the hint of hurt.

"It has a certain charm. I'll give you that. But after all, this isn't a fairy tale we're talking about. This is the rest of our lives."

Jud's heart started to pound again. Was it possible she was going to accept?

"This is the story we'll tell our grandchildren," she said cautiously and his heart gave a leap of joy when she nodded.

He grinned. "Got it." He leaned out the window. "Elijah, we'd like to go to the Tidal Basin, please."

The cherry blossoms were in bloom and the day was crystal clear with a warm breeze that promised days of unending spring to come. Jud and Grace strolled slowly along the Tidal Basin near the Jefferson Memorial.

"Better?" Jud asked taking Grace's hand.

"Much." She ducked her head, suddenly shy as it hit her anew that Jud was about to officially—and in person—ask her to marry him.

"I know we haven't known each other that long," he said, "and if you want a long engagement, I'll understand."

"Sometimes," Grace replied, "it's not the amount of time, but what's in your heart…and head."

"And what's in your heart and head, Grace?"

She paused for a moment under a canopy of white

and pink blossoms that floated gently down around them like a blessing from above. "I love you," she said simply, her eyes locked on his. "And you?"

"A wise woman once told me that God had created one true love for every person and that the challenge was to find that person. I'd like to think I can stop searching."

Tears wet her lashes. "Oh, Jud, just ask me."

Jud grinned and dropped to one knee. He pulled a small ring box from his pocket. "Mom," he explained with a sheepish grin, "put it in my suitcase before we left the farm."

Elijah watched them from his vantage point leaning against the side of the car.

"Looks to me, Lord, like our Gracie has got herself a keeper in this boy."

They'll be good for each other, he thought as he sipped his coffee. Good for others, too.

Elijah chuckled and then wiped away a tear with the back of one gnarled hand as he watched Jud get down on one knee. And when Grace cupped Jud's face between her hands and pulled him to his feet and kissed him, Elijah went for the handkerchief in his back pocket. "Match made in heaven this one—that's for sure."

Epilogue

The week leading up to the wedding was filled with showers and luncheons. It was as if everyone they knew was trying hard to make up for the fact that the groom was on assignment overseas. Jud was scheduled to arrive in the wee hours of the morning of their wedding day.

"I think I remember how this goes," he joked via cell phone during the rehearsal. "Dave, you are *not* to practice kissing my bride, understood?"

Grace's father had had his staff set up a speakerphone so that Jud could be as much a part of the festivities as possible. His voice crackled as the connection wavered, then recovered.

Bethany played her dual role of wedding coordinator and maid of honor to perfection. "So, Jud, this is your cue to come and stand with David and the minister." She cued the trio of musicians. "Can you hear that?"

"Roger," Jud replied. There was a loud crackle on his end.

"What was that?" Grace asked, her heart in her throat as his voice faded.

"We're moving back to base camp," he replied. "We hit a bump in the road and some of these wimps with me…"

"It was a crater," they heard someone protest.

Jud just laughed. "Don't listen to these guys, Gracie. Now let me hear that 'Wedding March.'"

Bethany cued the musicians and they played as she walked down the aisle in place of Grace. The only sound from Jud's end was the roar that they now knew was the vehicle's engine.

"Jud, you still there?" Gus Marlowe asked when the music ended and there still was no sound.

"Yeah." His voice sounded muffled. "Right here. Put Grace on and turn off the speaker."

Grace flew to the phone and waited until David had pushed the button to mute the speakerphone. Bethany herded everyone away to give her privacy.

"Jud?"

"How's everybody holding up?" he asked.

"Everyone's fine." She checked the dual watch he had given her when Millie gave him his first overseas assignment. One face gave her the time in Washington and the other the time wherever Jud was. "Are you sure you've got enough time to make that flight out? We can always postpone, Jud."

What were we thinking? It's not like there was any

great rush. I mean we love each other. What's six months or a year? All that matters is being together for the rest of our lives.

"You wouldn't be trying to get out of marrying me, would you?" She cherished the sound of laughter that came from Jud.

"Never. You're the one who keeps running halfway round the world."

"Last time without you, I promise. 'Whither I goest' and all that..."

"Did you get the story?"

"Got it. Filed it. Told Millie not to call me for two weeks. What about you? Please tell me Bethany's not planning to go on our honeymoon with us."

Grace actually giggled. "She is so busy matching half of D.C. to the other half that I honestly think she'll be relieved to check us off her list."

Over the last six months, their lives had taken a series of unexpected turns. Following the publication of Jud's story on the two senators' cooperative effort, Millie had promoted Jud to the news desk. His work had led him to assignments all over the world. So Grace had turned over her matchmaking duties to Bethany and gone with him. While he followed stories that had made him a household name back home, Grace visited hospitals, orphanages and local schools. In the process, she found her true calling—a love of working with disadvantaged children.

"Hey, Gracie! You still there?" Jud's voice was fading. The connection was weak.

"Right here," she answered, aware of the others turning as she raised her voice.

"What is it you and Bethany always say? See you in church? Well, if a garden is a church, I'll be waiting there tomorrow at the appointed hour. Don't be late. I love you."

And the line went dead.

The weather and setting on the day of her wedding could not have been more perfect. She and Jud had chosen his parents' farm for the ceremony. It was a golden autumn day—the very definition of an Indian summer day. The gardens had been transformed into a sanctuary to rival any cathedral.

Her gown hung on the closet door—a cloud of tulle and satin and tiny sequins that caught and reflected the morning light. She could hear the others stirring, her bridesmaids, who had spent the night in the attic dormitory, laughing and regaling each other with Grace stories. Jud's mom was bustling around in the kitchen below preparing breakfast in spite of the fact that everyone had told her they would be too excited to eat. No one said anything about the fact that the groom had not yet arrived.

Grace went through the morning in something of a daze. Her thoughts were on Jud and the moments they were about to share and the weeks and months and years ahead of them. After talking to him at the rehearsal, she had gone back to the room she was staying in—his room—to find a beautiful orchid plant in full bloom. Listen to your voice mail, read the card attached.

Grace had rummaged through her purse for her phone and flicked it on. There was a picture of Jud surrounded by smiling soldiers and holding a piece of cardboard with a crudely drawn heart that read "Grace + Jud 4-Ever."

She pressed the code to retrieve her voice mail.

"Grace, I know it was hard to talk with everyone around even after the speaker was turned off. Same thing at this end. The others are sleeping. We're about an hour from base—on schedule. Sweetheart, I cannot wait for us to get started with our life together. It's going to be so fantastic. I'll see you tomorrow, Grace, and every day for the rest of our lives."

Grace sat on the edge of the bed facing the closet where her gown hung. All that was left was to step into her wedding dress and shoes, let Bethany arrange her veil and wait for her cue. Grace walked over to the window and looked down on the garden below. Large wicker baskets filled with mums in every variety and color formed the backdrop for the altar where she and Jud would repeat their vows and dedicate their lives to each other.

She watched the red and burgundy leaves of a sheltering oak tree drift softly to the ground, like the rose petals Jud's niece would drop to herald Grace's walk down the aisle. She remembered the pink of the cherry blossoms that had cascaded around them the day Jud proposed.

"There's so much we can do," she whispered. "Thank You, God, for this man, for this life we are about to share."

Outside, she heard a car on the gravel drive. After a moment, she was aware of voices raised. She smiled and stepped into her gown. As she fumbled with the tiny buttons, she heard footsteps approaching, followed by a soft knock.

"Jud," she said happily. "Come in."

Her mom and Connie walked in together, Connie holding a portable phone. They were both smiling.

"There's a call for you," Connie said and handed her the phone.

"Gracie?" His voice was as clear and strong as if he were standing in front of her.

"Oh, Jud, don't tell me you're going to be late."

"Oh, ye of little faith. Look out the window," he said.

Grace moved to the window and there amid the flowers and the empty chairs to the right of the altar with David at his side stood Jud. He was still in fatigues and looked as if it had been a week since he slept, but he was there.

"Are we going to do this thing or not, lady?" she heard him ask over the phone as she read the words on his lips.

Grace gave a shriek of joy and dropped the phone. In her stocking feet, she ran from the room and down the stairs. She passed a blur of smiling faces—Jud's family, her family, their friends—on her way through the downstairs rooms and out the patio doors to the garden.

As soon as he saw her, Jud started to run toward her and they met halfway down the aisle. He caught her in his arms and lifted her, spinning round and round as leaves of red, purple and gold showered down around them.

Their mothers stood watching them from the window.

"A perfect match, wouldn't you say?" Catherine asked.

Connie shared one of the several tissues she'd been clutching from the moment they'd handed Grace the phone.

"Perfectly matched and perfectly blessed," she agreed.

Dear Reader,

Matchmaker, Matchmaker... is exactly that—a story in which each character makes a match that takes him or her to a new level. Of course, Jud and Grace find a love match, but beyond that, Jud reconnects with God and Grace finds a wonderful extended family through her match with Jud. Even the two senators make a match—one that will allow them to do even more good than each might have alone. Sometimes when you are writing or telling a story, there are these wonderful surprises. In this case, it was the realization that we have opportunities to connect—or make a match—every day. Maybe even several times a day. The stranger walking toward us on a busy street who seems troubled until we offer a smile and a greeting, or better yet, a compliment. I often practice this in my workplace, where stress-filled days can be the norm and I often see coworkers looking overwhelmed. I might say something like, "What a wonderful color that sweater is for you!" It's amazing to see the other person's worried frown relax and a smile take its place. In that sense, perhaps we are "momentary" matches for others—the exact person they needed to see or hear from. Is there someone you know who could use a lift? Could you make that simple gesture that would brighten someone's day or give a person the support and comfort needed? This book has taught me that matchmaking is not just about finding true love. It's about connections—with God and each other in every facet of our lives.

All the best to you,

Anna Schmidt

CHANGING HER HEART

BY

GAIL SATTLER

Meals were lonely for a single guy whose friends were getting married all around him. But Randy Reynolds knew his world had changed when Lacey Dachin started work at the shop next door. Could he convince Lacey his party-boy past was behind him?

Men of Praise: Faithful and strong, these men lead in worship and love.

Don't miss
CHANGING HER HEART
On sale February 2006
Available at your favorite retail outlet.

REQUEST YOUR FREE BOOKS!

2 FREE INSPIRATIONAL NOVELS
PLUS A
FREE
MYSTERY GIFT

Love Inspired

YES! Please send me 2 FREE Love Inspired® novels and my FREE mystery gift. After receiving them, if I don't wish to receive any more books, I can return the shipping statement marked "cancel." If I don't cancel, I will receive 4 brand-new novels every month and be billed just $3.99 per book in the U.S., or $4.74 per book in Canada, plus 25¢ shipping and handling per book and applicable taxes, if any*. That's a savings of over 20% off the cover price! I understand that accepting the 2 free books and gift places me under no obligation to buy anything. I can always return a shipment and cancel at any time. Even if I never buy another book from Steeple Hill, the two free books and gift are mine to keep forever.

113 IDN D74R 313 IDN D743

Name _____ (PLEASE PRINT) _____

Address _____ Apt. _____

City _____ State/Prov. _____ Zip/Postal Code _____

Signature (if under 18, a parent or guardian must sign)

Order online at www.LoveInspiredBooks.com

Or mail to Steeple Hill Reader Service™:

IN U.O.A
3010 Walden Ave.
P.O. Box 1867
Buffalo, NY 14240-1867

IN CANADA
P.O. Box 609
Fort Erie, Ontario
L2A 5X3

Not valid to current Love Inspired subscribers.

Want to try two free books from another series?
Call 1-800-873-8635 or visit www.morefreebooks.com

* Terms and prices subject to change without notice. NY residents add applicable sales tax. Canadian residents will be charged applicable provincial taxes and GST. This offer is limited to one order per household. All orders subject to approval. Credit or debit balances in a customer's account(s) may be offset by any other outstanding balance owed by or to the customer.

LIREG05

Love Inspired®

TITLES AVAILABLE NEXT MONTH

Don't miss these four stories in February

A HANDFUL OF HEAVEN by Jillian Hart
The McKaslin Clan

Hardworking single mother Paige McKaslin was the backbone that held her family together, but when the family diner burned down, it left her free to discover her own path...and a blossoming relationship with rancher Evan Thornton. Could it be that God still had some surprises in store for her?

AMAZING LOVE by Mae Nunn
Texas Treasures

Texas beauty Claire Savage learned a hard lesson the day her father left to pursue his selfish dreams. She never expected church newcomer and former rocker Luke Dawson's noble spirit to soothe her, yet could even his gentle touch curb her mistrust when his past resurfaced to threaten them both?

A MOTHER'S PROMISE by Ruth Scofield
Part of the NEW BEGINNINGS miniseries

A fresh start was hard for single mom Lisa Marley. Though she'd made her share of mistakes, all she wanted was a chance to raise her daughter. Widower Ethan Vance's deepening interest might just be the tie to bind them together...as a family.

CHANGING HER HEART by Gail Sattler
Men of Praise

When lovely Lacey Dachin signed on at the shop next door, it looked as if Randy Reynolds had found a potential lunch date...until she discovered his party-boy past. With his life in stand-up shape, the only thing that needed changing now was Lacey's mind.

LICNM0106